Three 1

MW01147956

Janice Magner

"After you read this book tell a friend to read it,
and tell that friend to tell a friend to read it,
and so on and so on and so on!
Great stories should be shared among great friends!"

Xlibris

publishing

To order additional copies of this book, contact:
Xlibris Corporation
1-888-795-4274
www.Xlibris.com
Orders@Xlibris.com
64651

Janice Magner's **Three Days of Darkness** is this summer's thriller—with characters right out of your own neighborhood or nearest church parish—a roller coaster ride from start to finish. A book to read and reread on the edge of your seat.

-Joanne Lewis-

A book to take cover with . . . prepare yourselves for the **Three Days of Darkness.**

-Jill Enrich-

Shocking and unnerving . . . could this really happen? Fear seized me at the turn of every page.

-Jim Szabo-

I couldn't put it down. Fast moving and compelling. Ms. Magner knows suspense and instills fear into her readers with ease.

-Anthony Desilva-

Will you be ready??? Research for yourselves the TRUE PROPHECY called the **Three Days of Darkness**. This prophecy is heading our way. Time is running out. Prepare for it now before it's too late.

Also by Janice Magner

Spite the Devil

Three Days of Darkness

Janice Magner

The story you're about to read is based on a true prophecy circulating in the Catholic Church. All of the prophecy is real and all the preparations should be addressed as forewarned. Mankind is heading into a very uncertain time in which a great chastisement will soon take place. Three quarters of the world's population will be annihilated and there will be such a wrath, such as no wrath ever before in all the ages, brought down to mankind as a great punishment and cleansing.

The remainder of the story is my interpretation of some things that could happen, but not necessarily what will happen. The characters are fictitious.

Dedication

I dedicate this book first and foremost to the Father,
Son & Holy Ghost and to the Immaculate Heart of Mary

Also to my dear & closest friends, John, Joanne & Jess

Special Acknowledgements

I wish to thank everyone who contributed
to the publication and promulgation of this book.

May God bless you one and all!

Chapter 1

It was an ordinary Sunday, in an extraordinary time. No one was prepared to hear the sermon Father McGrath was about to give. There was the usual sputter of coughs and pages turning in prayer books. Mrs. Sullivan cast a watchful eye on her fidgeting son James. Mr. Sullivan got ready to nod off for a quick nap. Mr. Nelson sneezed into his handkerchief and blew his nose. His wife Margaret cleared her throat to catch his attention and listen up. People were fumbling with their clothes, getting comfortable, ready to listen. Rick, my tall dark handsome husband, adjusted Rachel's hat as he rocked baby Kate in his arms and cast a smile in my direction. I told our son Daniel to stop pushing his brother Ricky and keep still. But no one was prepared for what came next.

The gospel for the day had already been read. Father McGrath looked grimly over his parishioners. He checked the microphone to be sure it was working. Then he began in the utmost serious tone we had ever heard him speak in.

"My dear brethren," he began. "It is of the utmost importance that you listen to everything I have to say with the utmost of interest and with keen remembrance so as to prepare for what lies ahead."

Rick looked over to me and smiled.

"Here we go again," he mumbled under a little grin.

But this wasn't going to be the usual sermon, where Father told us we were all bound for hell and would burn in the everlasting flames of damnation. This was going to be worse than that.

I sensed an urgency in Father's tone. I turned to Rick and whispered, "Be quiet. Let's hear what he has to say."

Father looked around the church. He waited until it was very quiet. Then he proceeded.

"There is a great prophecy circulating within the Catholic Church that may happen at any time now. I suggest you all prepare for it after you have heard everything I have to say. We're living in very dangerous times indeed," he paused looking the parish over and making sure he had everyone's attention.

"I am speaking about the prophecy called the *Three Days of Darkness*. This is not a new prophecy. It has been attributed to many saints and seers from the 1800's. Some think it was begun by Padre Pio, but he is not solely responsible for bringing its warning to the world. For your information, there was a Sister Marie Baourdi of France and Saint Hildegard of Germany who prophesied about this chastisement. Pere Lamy a French Priest spoke of this prophecy. A stigmatized Nun in Italy warned about it, along with countless others. They have done so, not to frighten you, but rather so you can prepare yourselves for it, to sanctify yourselves and be ever ready for it in the state of grace. No one knows the hour in which this will take place, but it will happen."

You could hear a pin drop as Father looked around the church to make sure people were listening. He continued. "We are already living in rather questionable times. These seers warned of impending signs that will prelude the actual *Three Days of Darkness*. They said to look for great earthquakes, huge tidal waves, hurricanes, tornadoes, floods, epidemics, crop failures, downfalls of governments and wars, lack of respect for authorities, breakdown of family life, rampant adultery, immorality, indecency, irreverence and immodesty in Church, neglect of holy conduct on Sundays and lack of concern for our neighbors."

"Look around you! Aren't these things in the news? Haven't we seen the changes in the weather patterns? Aren't there earthquakes and hurricanes and tornadoes and floods happening all around us? Look at the indecency everywhere! You can't turn on the TV without seeing something lewd. The book stores are filled with forbidden books. Magazines and newspapers at the check out aisles in the supermarkets display all kinds of immodest pictures with stories flashing about immoral behavior. These are just a few of the impending things the seers warned about."

"But what proof, you may ask, do we have that an impending chastisement is at hand? A prodigy will occur showing every person how they have offended the Almighty God! This will cause such an intense suffering that many souls will wish to die, but none will. And again, a miracle will take place on the feast day of a *young martyr of the Eucharist* before this chastisement will happen. The Holy Father will see it no matter where he is in the world. This miracle will be announced eight days before it occurs, after which God will leave a sign for its memory. A luminous cross will also appear in the sky. Everyone will have time to reflect on the significance of that cross! It will remind the faithful why a Savior came into the world. The punishment shall not happen without previous warnings!"

"What will happen after this, you may be wondering? Beware of a bitterly cold night and look to see thunderbolts rain down from the skies, stars will quake and heavenly bodies will be restless! There won't be any light! There will only be total darkness. Hell will be emptied out. Demons will roam the earth doing harm to many souls. People will die from fear! Fire will envelope the earth. Many souls will burn! This will be a chastisement like no other before and will effect the entire globe! Lucifer will seem to be triumphant, but God will reclaim the earth."

People began to gasp at the serious nature with which he spoke. They wondered if what he said was true or had he just gone mad? Would this really happen? Would it happen soon? What could they do to stop it from happening?

"Pray to save yourselves! Pray to save others! Pray that these days will be shortened! But you can't pray against these days, they will come! As soon as you see these disturbed signs on a very cold night, go inside and lock all your doors and windows and cover them! Don't look outside. Don't go outside. And don't talk to anyone outside. Anyone who looks or goes out will die immediately! We are not permitted to witness the wrath of God. You will be in total blackness. The only thing that will give you light is a blessed candle. Light it immediately. Once lit, nothing will put them out in the houses of believers. If you are a scoffer or do not believe your candles will not burn!"

"It is best to have a good supply of holy water in your homes. Sprinkle it freely around the house, especially at the doors and windows. Bless yourselves and drink it! Keep a supply of nonperishable foods on hand, along with blankets and water. Don't count on any utilities, they won't work. Leave enough food and water for your pets outside to last for three days. God will preserve the property of the elect."

"Then pray! Pray as you have never prayed before! Pray with outstretched arms! Pray prostrate on the floor! Plead for many souls to be saved! Pray your rosaries! Those who are traveling at the time and unable to get to shelter will die as martyrs and taken to Heaven if they have been good. Those who disregard this warning and advice will die *instantly!* These days will come! Make no mistake about it!"

"When the chastisement is over, no ungodly person will be left on the earth! Three quarters of the population will be annihilated! Everything will be purified. Then the sun will shine again and there will be peace on earth. Some nations will disappear entirely and the face of the world will be changed. Those who have survived the three days will come to find no more large industries or big businesses. People will return to the land. Holy Church will rise again!"

"And I say to those who do survive this ordeal, get down on your knees and thank God for His protection!"

No one said a word. Everyone was still. Father looked around at everyone's faces. No one knew what he would say next.

"Get in and remain in the state of grace today! God has promised to protect the just. If you are in the state of grace you have nothing to fear. Have recourse to the Blessed Virgin Mary, pray your rosary! Call on Her for assistance. Come to more than one Mass if possible. Offer this up for poor souls and make sacrifices for them. You should already be doing these things as practicing Catholics! If you aren't there's no better time to begin than right now! Have your homes blessed by a priest and always keep holy water on hand, along with blessed wax candles, blessed palms, blessed crucifixes, and images of Our Lord and Blessed Mother."

"It could happen any day now. Pray my dear people, pray the Rosary! May God bless you all."

With that Father turned off his microphone and proceeded back to the altar to finish Mass. Everyone looked at one another in shock and disbelief. No one knew what to make of what he had just said. Everyone rose for the Credo and then focused keenly on the rest of the Mass.

When Mass was over people filed quietly out of the church. Some were shaking their heads. Some had big smiles on their faces. Some hurried away to get into their cars and drive home.

"What did you think about what Father said?" I asked Rick as he strapped Katie into her car seat.

"It's a lot of hogwash!" Rick laughed.

"Be careful! Father warned those that scoff or don't believe will die instantly!"

"You don't really believe everything he said, do you?" Rick shut his door and started up the van.

"I do. There was something about the urgency with which he spoke that frightened me. So many seers spoke about the same thing happening from different parts of the globe, at different times. How did they all know this event was going to happen without having heard one another speak about it? There was no TV back then. How would they communicate news like this to various countries?"

Rick couldn't answer with any certainty.

"I don't know. So what if the prophecy is true. Do you really think it's going to happen in our time? Natural catastrophes have been going on for ages. What makes today any different from any other time?"

"Disasters are more wide spread today. Look at all the storms heading up the coast. There are so many tropical storms and hurricanes. Look at all the tornadoes tearing up the midwest. Look at all the dormant volcanoes now on the verge of erupting and those that already have. Look at the morals of people today. No one is shamed at their behavior. Look how they dress and behave. Look at all the babies being aborted and the constant display of provocative behavior on TV like Father said. Those things can't be denied. They are happening."

"But that doesn't mean it's the end of the world!" Rick chuckled.

"It's not the end. It's a warning. It's a punishment about to happen. Punishments have happened before. Noah had his flood. Sodom & Gomorrah had their chastisement. Why should it be any different for us? Don't you think God is pretty angry with the world today? There was such an urgency in Father's voice."

I turned to Rick and pleaded, "You have to believe him! You must! I couldn't go through what's going to happen alone. Tell me you do believe him!"

Rick's expression turned a little more serious. He heard the concern in my voice. The children were getting a little frightened.

"All right, all right," he kept driving. "Maybe there's something to it. So what are we going to do?"

"We'll have to prepare for it. We'll have to be ready. I'll stock the little laundry room downstairs with canned goods and some blankets. There aren't any windows down there so we won't need to cover anything or be tempted to look out. I'll have to get some blessed candles and I'll make sure we have an ample supply of holy water. We have plenty of rosaries and crosses in the house. I'd like Father to come out just the same and bless it anyway."

We drove home the rest of the way in silence. Father's sermon was surely something to think about.

When we arrived home, the children ran off to play on the swings in the yard as Rick and I scrambled to get into the house.

"I want to call Joanne and tell her all about this," I headed for the telephone in the den.

Joanne and her husband John were both very close friends of ours and their daughter Jess was Ricky's age. We all got along famously. While I got on the phone, Rick headed for the Sunday paper and sat down on the couch in the living room to read the sports section.

"Hell-o, Joanne?" I asked. "We just got home from church today and there's something I want to tell you about. Father McGrath had the strangest sermon today."

I began to relay the story all over again in great detail to my dear friend.

"Isn't that odd, you should mention this? I had the strangest dream last night about people running for their lives, panicking in the streets, and it was dark, just like it was night!" Joanne told me.

"I don't want to scare the kids, but I don't think we should take any chances. I'm going to have Father bless our house. And I'm going to get some beeswax candles and have him bless them as well."

"Will you get a few candles for me too? I'll pay you for them," Joanne was on the same wave length.

"Will do," I replied.

I hadn't noticed but the sky had darkened outside and I could hear the rumble of thunder. All at once the kids were screaming and running in the house.

"There's a storm brewing Joanne. I have to run."

"Let me know about the candles," she added and then hung up.

I hung up the phone too and went to look out the front door. The sky was turning black with huge storm clouds rolling in. Suddenly Rick was behind me.

"Looks like a whopper of a storm!" he grinned.

"Do you think we'll loose power?" Daniel asked me.

"We might, honey. But there's nothing to worry about. Go get a couple of flashlights now so we'll be ready." Then I turned to Rick, "Maybe I should get a few candles and some matches just to be on the safe side."

"WOOOOO!" he teased me.

"Stop it!" I chided him back. "I told Joanne everything Father told us. She believes! She wants some blessed candles too. It can't hurt to be ready. You can't be too careful."

Just then a bright light pierced the darkness and a large clap of thunder crackled through the air.

"We better shut the door. Where did you put those candles?" I said shuffling through the hallway.

The kids were already having a ball shining the flashlights through the house all over the walls and the ceilings.

"I want a turn!" Ricky whined at his brother.

"Me first!" Rachel demanded.

A small argument started to break out when suddenly a bolt of lightening burst from the sky and a huge rumble of thunder pounded the entire house. The lights went out.

"Just in time!" I smiled as I found the candles and some matches.

The children all screamed.

"There's nothing to worry about," I put my arms around them. "It's only a storm. It will pass. Before you know it the sun will shine again and you can go out and play."

◎⌇◎

A few houses down, in a split level style house, Mr. Nelson hurried to close the windows while his wife Margaret lit a few candles.

"What do you make of it?" she joined her husband.

"It's pretty nasty out there," Mr. Nelson turned around heading for the upstairs rooms. The rain began to pour. "Make sure you check the kitchen window!" he called back to his wife.

When they both had secured the house, they sat down quietly in the living room together.

"It's kind of eerie, after hearing what Father had to say today, about the darkness and now this storm . . ." Margaret trailed off.

Another clap of thunder and lightening shook their house.

"It does seem very coincidental," Mr. Nelson put his arm around his wife. "But I wouldn't get too worried about all that right now."

"Just the same, I think we should do something to be ready. I still have those blessed candles from when Clare was sick, before she died. God rest her soul. Remember we had them burning for her as we said prayers?"

"A lot of good they did her. She died anyway," Mr. Nelson sneered.

"She was old. It was her time to go. I miss her still . . ." Margaret trailed off again.

❧

The Sullivan's lived four blocks away from the Nelson's house. They were a rowdy bunch, all eight of them. There was Patrick and Edward, Chris was the oldest, Colleen and Mary Alice. And who could forget James, the youngest and the most mischievous. He was forever being chided by the stern Mrs. Sullivan who was careful about her children's behavior.

"Stop swinging that flashlight at your brother!" Mrs. Sullivan yelled at James. "Do you want to poke an eye out?"

"Do as your mother says!" Mr. Sullivan chimed in. "I'm not driving to the hospital tonight through a storm like this one! You can bleed to death right here!"

A clap of thunder and lightening rocked the house like no other had done before. It silenced the whole family at once.

"Let's all say the rosary," Mrs. Sullivan took the rosary beads she always carried with her out of her pocket. She led the bunch of them to the family room, to gather around the lighted candles she had placed there and began, "In the name of the Father, and of the Son, and of the Holy Ghost, Amen . . ."

❧

It was a pretty wicked storm, with the wind howling, limbs breaking from trees and power lines knocked down all over town. But everyone survived it. Somehow we managed to get through the night, although the kids were restless. And just as I had foretold, it passed. The sun was up and shining the next day.

As I did the morning dishes Rick gave me a goodbye kiss and left for work. The kids all ran outside to play on the swings. I wiped off the countertops and poured myself another cup of coffee as I looked out the window watching my children play. I turned on the little television on my countertop to watch the news.

"There's been a drive-by shooting. Two people are dead. Two others are being hospitalized. If anyone has any information connected with this crime please call . . ."

I switched the channel.

A provocative young woman was running her fingers through a half dressed young man's hair. He embraced her back.

"That's pretty steamy for so early in the morning," I switched the channel.

"Looks like another scorcher in the midwest again. No hope of rain in sight. Farmers are frantic trying to salvage crops. While the rain just won't stop in the southern states . . ."

I turned the TV off. There was nothing of interest on it.

I picked up the paper as I sipped my coffee. The headlines were in bold print, "Abortion Clinic Under Attack!" Someone had planted an explosive in the front of the building. At least half a dozen people had been hurt. I put the paper down and looked out the window again at my children playing. I sipped my coffee peacefully. The phone rang.

"Hell-o?" I answered it.

"Hi Jill," it was Joanne. "When do you think you're going to get the blessed candles?"

"Oh, thanks for reminding me. I'll call Father today. I'm going to see if he can come out to bless the house too. Do you need any holy water?"

"I always keep a jug of that around. I told John all about what you told me and he just laughed. He doesn't believe a word of it."

"Rick was the same way. It must be a manly thing."

As I looked out the window I noticed Rachel fighting with Ricky.

"Joanne, let me call you back. There's a small battle brewing outside!"

"All right," she understood completely. "Talk to you later."

I brought out a pitcher of lemonade and a huge helping of fresh baked brownies and the children immediately changed their behavior from anger to enjoyment. I picked up a ball that had been tossed aside after the argument and yelled back over my shoulder, "You have to share."

When I got back inside the house I searched for my address book to look up Father McGrath's telephone number. I was happy to hear his voice when he answered the phone.

"Yes Father, we'd like you to come out to bless our house. When do you think you would be able to come? All right then. We'll look forward to seeing you Saturday. God bless you too. Oh Father, by the way, I almost forgot. I'm going to need a few blessed candles too. And if it isn't a big imposition would you be able to bring us a jug of holy water? That would be wonderful. We look forward to seeing you Saturday. God bless you."

While I had the time, I decided to go on a scavenger hunt looking for things we would need to survive the *Three Days of Darkness*. I grabbed some blankets from the upstairs hall closet and brought them downstairs to the laundry room. I tried straightening the little room up so that it would be a comfortable living room. Next, I looked for a spare box of matches. We were going to need them to light the blessed candles. There was an ample supply of canned vegetables, tuna, baked beans, ravioli, and peanut butter for the kids on the shelves that lined the small room. I also stocked other foods down there like crackers, cake and cookie mixes and spaghetti. We used a lot of things from that pantry on a daily basis.

"I better get a manual can opener. Father said the utilities aren't going to work. No electricity."

We had one buried in the kitchen drawer that I took with me to the laundry room. Then I gathered a wooden crucifix and hung it on the wall down there. I also found a small statue of the Blessed Mother which I placed on the top shelf over the canned goods.

"There now," I said aloud. "What else do we need?"

It suddenly occurred to me that it was going to be a very long three days. Besides praying we would need some spiritual books to read and focus on. I ran to the living room to grab our family Bible. I also picked up a few books with stories of the saints in them too.

"This should do it!" I brought everything downstairs.

"What's for lunch?" Rachel came inside wondering. She noticed me bringing things down to the laundry room.

"What are you doing?" she asked me.

"Nothing honey, I'm just getting prepared."

"Prepared for what?"

"Just getting prepared," I tried to change the subject not wanting to scare her. "Do you and your brothers want some hot dogs for lunch?"

"That sounds great!" she hollered.

Just then I thought I heard the baby cry, "Sounds like Katie needs a bottle too."

I hurried up the stairs to pick up baby Kate and Rachel ran outside to call her brothers to come and wash up for lunch. As I sat Kate in her high chair at the kitchen table the phone rang. It was Mrs. Nelson.

"Hell-o Margaret, what can I do for you?" I said.

"My husband wants to know if Rick could stop by and help him with a big tree limb that came down in our yard from the big storm last night."

"We don't have any plans for tonight. Would it be okay if he stopped by after dinner?" I asked her.

"That would be wonderful Jill," she became quite serious, "Did you believe everything Father McGrath warned us about on Sunday? I mean, it sounded so strange. Do you really think we may have a chastisement soon?"

"I'm not sure Margaret, but I'd hate to be caught unprepared for it. I called Father McGrath this morning to have him come out to bless our house. I asked him to bring some holy water and blessed candles also. In fact, I told a good friend of mine about this whole thing and she wants some candles too."

"Then I'm not crazy for believing what Father said?"

"If you are, then I am as well! It can't hurt to be ready. Always be prepared! That's what they taught us in the scouts."

"You're right," she seemed more at ease. "I think I'll call Maureen Sullivan too. She was talking to my Don about it, but Don didn't take her too serious. I don't have to worry about blessing our house. We had it blessed a few years back when Clare died you know. Father had come out to visit us back then."

"Sounds like you're all set then. Do you have blessed candles and holy water?"

"Oh yes, I have plenty of holy water. And we have the blessed candles here from Clare too. God rest her soul."

"You miss her don't you?" I could hear it in her voice.

"Yes, I do. She was the last member of my family to go. I'm the only one left."

"Don't worry, Margaret. I'm sure she's looking down on you from Heaven and smiling all the while."

"You're probably right, dear. But I do miss her," she changed the subject. "I'll let Don know that Rick will be over after dinner with a saw. Thanks for being such good neighbors. We'll see him later."

Then she hung up the phone.

I got back to making lunch and feeding baby Kate.

Chapter 2

Father McGrath arrived early Saturday morning with an ample supply of holy water and a case load of blessed white candles. I greeted him at the door while the kids stood around curious as to why he had come.

"Thank you so much for coming Father. We know how busy you are but we really would like our house blessed," I began.

"Why do we need our house blessed?" Ricky asked.

"Run along now," I scooted the children to go out and play.

"Good morning Father," Rick joined me welcoming the tired priest into our living room. "Let me take that," Rick grabbed a gallon-sized jug filled with holy water from him and a case full of blessed candles.

"Those aren't all for you," Father interjected. "I promised a few to the Sullivan's. I'll be stopping there after you. They want their house blessed as well. And the parish has been inundated with phone calls to have me come bless houses. I'm glad people are paying attention to what I said."

I cast a watchful eye at Rick.

"You know one of the things I didn't mention at Mass when I was talking about this prophecy was that more men will perish in this ordeal than women. I'm not sure why but . . ." he looked at Rick. "Let's begin in the living room."

Father took his stole out and wrapped it around his neck. Then he opened his prayer book and set a small bottle of holy water aside on a table. He began to read the prayers aloud. When he finished reading he sprinkled the room with holy water and then walked through the entire house continuing to sprinkle the water in every room.

"Father, would you be sure and bless our laundry room. I've prepared it . . . just in case."

Father blessed it for us then turned to be on his way.

"You can have six candles. If you need more, you can pick them up on Sunday at the bookstore. I'll be on my way now. I have quite a few more stops to make. God bless you," Father closed the door behind him.

Picking up three candles I turned to Rick, "We'll keep three of these. I'll give three to John and Joanne. More men will die than women? I wonder if that has anything to do with their not believing in this prophecy."

Rick just looked at me as I headed for the laundry room to place the candles next to the matches on the shelf down there.

"Would you bring the holy water too please?" I added.

Joanne was happy to hear I had gotten her three blessed candles when I telephoned her that same day.

"Why don't you come by for a nice cup of tea later on and I'll give them to you?" I asked her.

"I'd love to. John is cutting the grass and Jess would love to play with Rachel and Ricky. What's a good time to stop by?" she asked me.

"Come by around two. I'll have Katie down for a nap by then and the house will be fairly quiet."

"See you then."

Rick decided to cut the grass too. Almost everyone in the neighborhood was out with a lawn mower that Saturday. Seems the rain had spurted the grass to grow.

After doing loads of laundry and cleaning the house, I put Katie down for a nap with her bottle and Rachel ran outside to play with her brothers and wait for Jess to arrive. I got out some pretty little tea cups and set the kitchen table with my fancy spoons and floral finger dishes. I had baked some homemade raspberry crumb bars and set them out in the middle of everything.

Just then the doorbell rang. Joanne and Jess had arrived. Joanne was holding some fresh cut flowers from her garden in her arms as she told Jess to go around back and play with the others.

"These are for you!" she outstretched her arms and leaned in for a kiss.

"You didn't have to do that! They're so beautiful! Are they from your garden?" I asked her.

She nodded yes and came inside. I hurried to get a tall vase to put the very colorful flowers in. Then I turned on the stove to heat the whistling tea kettle for our tea.

"Don't let me forget to give you the blessed candles before you leave," I mentioned.

"How much do I owe you?" she asked me.

"Nothing! I just want you to be safe. This is really going to be something if it happens in our lifetime!" The tea kettle started to whistle and I got up to pour the water into our tea cups.

"It sure will be. You know after I spoke to you about all this, I did a little research to try and find out more about a young martyr of the Holy Eucharist," Joanne jumped in.

"What did you find?" I was curious.

"Well, back in the 1300's there was a little girl by the name of Imelda who desired very much to receive the Holy Eucharist. She wasn't yet the proper age to partake of this sacrament. You had to be at least fourteen years of age but she requested to receive it at five years of age! It's kind of a long story, so I'll cut to the chase. After a long ordeal of cutting red tape, she finally did get permission to receive the Host. But she died of love that very day right after she received it! Poor little thing. Pope Leo XII venerated her as a Blessed in 1826. She had two feast days, May 12 and September 16, but they are no longer officially observed in the Church. Pope St. Pius V declared Blessed Imelda the Patroness of First Communicants."

"There's another Saint of the Eucharist, a Saint Tarcisius. He is the Patron of First Communicants. He lived during the third or fourth century. He was only twelve years old when he was martyred while carrying the Holy Eucharist. His feast day is August 15."

"They were both martyrs of the Eucharist and both very young when they died. It would be very odd to have a bitterly cold day in August, perhaps even in May, but it wouldn't be too unlikely to have a cold snap in September. It does get rather chilly some nights in the autumn."

"Yes, maybe it would arouse people if a bitterly cold night occurred when it shouldn't, don't you think?" I questioned.

"You may have something there. I shutter to think of it. What's the date today? August isn't that far away."

"It's July 31st," I cautioned her.

We finished our tea discussing the matter thoroughly. I even showed Joanne our laundry room complete with every modern convenience. Well, not exactly. We had a hand held can opener just in case.

"I hope the kids will be comfortable down here. I'm stocking up on ravioli and peanut butter and crackers for them."

Joanne told me she was busy preparing things in her own house too. They were going to use their family room. The windows had blinds and long drapes so they wouldn't be tempted to look outside. She felt they would endure the ordeal best in that room, should darkness come upon them suddenly.

Meanwhile, down the road a bit Mr. Nelson was out gardening in his yard when a neighbor approached him for a little chat.

"That was some storm the other night!" Mr. Enrich began.

"It certainly was. It knocked a big tree limb down on this strip of my garden. What a mess cleaning it up!" Mr. Nelson looked up at him.

"We lost power for a while," Mr. Enrich continued.

"So did we. Margaret was starting to get alarmed thinking it was the beginning of the *Three Days of Darkness*."

"Come again, Don. What was that?"

"The *Three Days of Darkness* . . . haven't you heard about them?" Mr. Nelson looked up again.

"No. What's that all about?"

Mr. Nelson put his gardening tools down a minute and wiped some sweat off of his forehead. He began to explain about the foreboding prophecy.

"It's been circulating in the Catholic Church since the 1800's. Father McGrath thinks there's some urgency to prepare for it right away. Margaret is taking it pretty seriously."

"I don't believe in that stuff, do you? It sounds too far fetched," he laughed.

Margaret over heard their conversation and came out of the house with a blessed candle. She reached out her hand to Mr. Enrich, "Go on, take this. It's a blessed candle. You never know when you're going to need it."

Mr. Enrich stopped laughing not wanting to make fun of his friends, but still not believing a word they said. He took the candle, "I'll take it. But it'll just be another item in our house that collects dust!"

Margaret scolded him, "Dave, this is serious business! You better change your mind. Father warned us that the candles won't light in the house of a scoffer. I'd hate to think of what will become of you."

"All right, all right. I'll keep it handy."

But he had no intention of changing his position on the topic. Margaret asked if they'd like some cool lemonade. It was a very hot day and Mr. Nelson had been out for a while working in that hot sun. He nodded he could use a cool drink.

"I'll only be a minute," Margaret walked back to the house.

⌒⌒

"I'd better get going," Joanne sipped the last of her tea. We're going over to my in-law's for a cookout. I'm running a little late. Thanks for the tea and candles."

"No problem," I cleared the table putting the cups in the sink.

"I'll call you tomorrow. Maybe we can go shopping next week and grab some lunch," Joanne kissed me goodbye.

"Sounds like a plan. I'd love to," I waved goodbye to her as she got Jess into the car and drove off. Rick came into the house.

"I'm thirsty. What do we have to drink?" he asked.

"There's a gallon of fruit punch in the refrigerator or you can have some iced tea."

"I'll pass on the fruit punch. Where's the ice tea?"

"I'll get you some."

He was sweating profusely.

"Why don't you go up and take a nice cool shower first?"

"Okay," he grinned and kissed me. "I'll be right down."

I went back to the kitchen and turned on the little TV on my countertop. I kept one eye on what was happening, and kept another eye on my kids playing happily in the yard. I began to wash the dishes in the sink.

"Good afternoon. It's July 31ˢᵗ. Here's what's in the news . . ." the TV trailed off as I looked out the window while I washed the dishes.

Rick came into the room, "That shower felt great!" He was much cooler now. "Where's that ice tea?" he opened the refrigerator and took the watermelon pitcher out to pour himself a glass.

Just then the kids came running in all at once. "Mommy! Mommy! We're hot! It's too hot! Can we have some ice cream?"

I turned around drying my hands in a dish towel when Rick ran over to the TV to turn the volume up a bit, "Quiet! I want to hear what they're saying."

"Come on guys," I motioned the kids to go wash up and told them I'd get them some ice cream.

"Would you look at that?" Rick couldn't believe his eyes. There was a devastating earthquake in Indonesia. Thousands were missing. Damage was extensive. Hundreds were killed. It was a horrific sight. But just as they finished with that story another flash of news came on.

"Haleakala is beginning to erupt! Thousands are evacuating. This volcano has been dormant for centuries! People are fleeing the island."

Still more devastating news flashed over the airwaves.

"Wild fires burn out of control in the southwest, while farmers pray for rain in the midwest. Farmers fear a poor harvest from lack of rain. It's been the worst year on record. Food prices will soar if this weather pattern doesn't change. There could be wide spread famine. And there's flooding again on the east coast. Rain continues to pound the whole coastline. Washington is under two feet of water! Everything is at a standstill . . ."

"It's just like a three ring circus! It's all over the place! Look at everything happening!" Rick began to take some credence in the prophecy seeing so many signs occurring everywhere and all at once!

"Why don't you turn that off now? We see the signs. We've prepared for the worst. What did Father say? He asked us to pray. But no matter, these days will come. Why don't we pray a rosary that the days will be shortened?"

I gave my kids some ice cream cones and sent them back out to play. Rick and I sat down in the living room and began our rosary in earnest.

☙

Mrs. Sullivan was out hanging clothes on the line when her little boy Jimmy came running by and tripped pulling a newly washed sheet to the ground with him. "James Patrick Sullivan!" she exploded. "Just wait 'til I get my hands on you young man!" He ran off again before she could catch him.

Mr. Sullivan was trimming the hedges when he noticed his son run by. Mrs. Sullivan was calling after him, but no one could hear her with the hedge clippers going. She finally caught up to her husband just as their next door neighbor Ed King came by with some startling news.

"Hell-o Maureen, Sean. I just wanted to stop by and tell you there's another storm heading up the coast. Our cellar is already flooded pretty high. Can I bother you for a helping hand? We've got a few pumps going but I think we may need to bail out as well."

"Sure Ed, no problem," Mr. Sullivan put the hedge clippers down immediately and ran off with his neighbor to lend a helping hand. Maureen just stood there watching them go and picked up the clippers before her boys might get into mischief with them. She looked up at the sky already beginning to darken again with thunderclouds. She headed back to their house.

"Better get the wash in," she complained. "No use having to wash it all over again."

That very same night, when the kids were all snug in their beds and the house was quiet, I got into bed myself for a well deserved night's rest. No sooner had my head hit the pillow then I was fast asleep.

All of a sudden I was standing in the streets looking at the horizon that was slowly filling up the sky with what looked like black ink! Everyone was staring and pointing to it, a phenomenon no one could explain. The sky was being soaked up into this black ink. Darkness was beginning to engulf everything.

I ran for my children and to as many people as I could, I screamed, "Run for shelter!" But no one would listen. They just kept staring at the sky.

I grabbed my children and ran into our house scrambling to get into our laundry room and lock the door. A couple of people joined us as I tried frantically to explain the *Three Days of Darkness* to them as quickly as I could. Then everything went black! I screamed out loud!

"Wake up! Wake up!" Rick was shaking me. "You must have had a bad dream!"

I stirred for a moment, "It was so real! I could see the sky turning black all along the horizon . . ."

The next day was Sunday and everyone was back in church. It was another hot humid day. The only thing the rain did was flood. It did nothing to cool things off. Father wiped his brow before beginning his sermon. He checked to see that the microphone was on.

"Good morning, brethren. It's going to be another hot one, so I'll keep my sermon short this week. I'd like to continue with what I spoke about last week, the *Three Days of Darkness*. I was happy to hear so many of you are taking what I said quite seriously. But there's more to it. So please, I beg of you, pay attention."

"I didn't mention the fact last week that there will be more men who will die from this chastisement than women. I'm not sure why that will be. But if it is because men don't believe this prophecy, then I implore you to truly give a listen. Unfortunately, I must add, some children will die as well and will be taken up to Heaven to spare them the horror of these days."

"Look at the signs in just this past week alone that point to every impending sign these seers have previously spoken about. There are increasing disturbances on land, at sea and in the air! Earthquakes, floods, famine, volcanoes erupting, it's ubiquitous!"

"Prepare yourselves! Prepare your homes if you have not already done so! When this bitterly cold night comes it will bring with it total blackness! There will be no light from anywhere, except your blessed candles."

"Hell will be emptied! Not a single demon will be left in hell! These demons will appear in the most frightening forms and will fill the air with pestilence and poisonous gases. There will be terrifying apparitions that will scare people to death from fear and despair! The wicked people will behold the Divine Heart of Our Lord. Special angels will stand ready to execute those who mock God and will not believe in these revelations."

"There will be great hurricanes of fire that will pour forth from Heaven and cover the earth. Fear will seize every man at this sight and there will be great cries of lamentation as they burn like withered grass in the open fields!"

No one moved. There was not a sound in church that day. Everyone's eyes and ears were on Father.

He continued, "Go inside your houses! Lock your doors and windows! Do not look out! Don't talk to anyone outside! Hear me! The tricks of the devil are cunning and deadly. Think back to the Garden of Eden and Adam and Eve. Eve's first mistake was that she talked to the serpent. If she never engaged in a conversation with that wicked one she may have spared countless generations all this. Pray! That's all you must do! Pray and read spiritual books! Keep plenty of books on hand. Read your Bibles!"

"Pray the rosary. Our Blessed Mother obtained from Jesus a promise, to those who recite the rosary, that they will have intercessors from the entire Celestial Court to assist them during their life and at the hour of their death. Have recourse to the Blessed Mother. Wear the Brown Scapular and gain the Sabbatine Privilege! Our Lady promised that those who wear this scapular and recite the prayers attached to it will be rescued from Purgatory the Saturday following their death."

"Be enrolled in and wear the Miraculous Medal which bestows great graces. Wear the St. Benedict medal, which is the highest indulgenced medal of the church. St. Benedict is a powerful saint often called upon during exorcisms to fight the devil. So is Saint Michael, call on him for assistance. Shout out ejaculations such as, '*Who is like unto God?*'"

"Have recourse to Saint Joseph. The devils flee in fear of him just hearing his name. St. Joseph is always near the Blessed Mother because it was given to him the duty to take care of Her. He is a very powerful saint. Do not forget him in your trials."

"Saint Athanasius told us that the devils fear Psalm 67 most! Say it out loud and often! '*Let God arise, and let His enemies be scattered, and let them that hate Him flee from before His face!*' This will compel the demons to take flight from you. Use it against your adversary."

"My dear people, we do not know when this event will take place, but if you listen to the gospels and see that the signs are all at hand, you can't help but prepare for these days that are so close by."

"I don't know what else to warn you about, except perhaps one more final bit of advice. Discouragement is the finest tool of the devil. It gives him an opening wedge. Do not give into it! Persevere in prayer to keep the devil at bay. Remember

God loves each and every one of you. He wants you to join Him in His kingdom. The devil does not love you. He wants you to perish in his kingdom. But remember this, no one goes to hell unless you will it! You can not be dragged down to hell without your own consent. Don't be tempted to have anything to do with the devil. Don't look outside! Don't talk to anyone outside! He is your adversary. He is waiting for you to slip and fall. Hear me and keep away from his tricks! May God bless all of you."

Father turned off his microphone and took his place back in front of the altar to recite the Credo. Katie began to cry for her bottle. Rick quickly picked her up and silenced her with it. The other children sat very quietly as the entire church stood helplessly watching and listening to the rest of the Mass.

"Dóminus vobíscum," Father finished.

"Et cum spíritu tuo," the altar boys echoed back.

We left church that day feeling a little more educated and accepting the fact that we had been graciously warned. I thought about how many wouldn't know what to do when the actual occurrences would begin to manifest. I thought about those who would scoff at this matter and those who would be lost traveling or in their cars at the time. Rick was beginning to come around too. I think the more he heard Father speak about this, the more he became aware and less ignorant. We drove home in silence.

It was a very hot August 1ˢᵗ that Sunday. I turned on the sprinkler to water the lawn as the kids got their bathing suits on and had a go at running through it. Rick decided to stay inside where it was air conditioned and watch the baseball game on TV. I decided to bake a blueberry coffee cake. Life seemed good and peaceful.

While my cake was baking, I decided to do a little more research about Saint Tarcisius on the internet. It was just as Joanne had said. It happened in the third or fourth century. He was only a boy of twelve years of age. He was on his way to give the Holy Eucharist to some prisoners who were being held and persecuted for practicing Christianity. Caught off guard, some pagans held him up and demanded to see his precious treasure. When Saint Tarcisius refused to show them the Holy Eucharist they began to throw stones and sticks at him. Saint Tarcisius died from their cruelty but when they turned him over seeking the Host they could not find it.

The buzzer was ringing and my cake was done. Rick called for me to come check it. The house smelled great filled with a buttery sweet flavor. I poked a toothpick in the cake to check for doneness. It baked perfectly. It was ready to come out of the oven. Grabbing a set of pot holders I quickly scooped the pan out of the stove and cooled the cake down on a wire rack.

"That smells great!" Rick was ready for a piece.

"Give it a little while to cool down a bit," I cautioned him.

"What should we do in the meantime?" Rick came over to me wrapping me in his arms.

"What did you have in mind?" I giggled.

Just then the front door burst open and Daniel came rushing in to use the bathroom. The rest of the children followed him smelling the cake.

"Is the cake ready yet?" Rachel asked anxiously.

"It smells so good!" Ricky added.

"Just a few more minutes and everyone can have a piece. So much for what we can do in the meantime," I smiled at my husband.

Rick went back to the living room to watch his game.

The telephone rang. It was Joanne.

"I've looked high and low for some religious objects and all I could come up with was a crucifix. We're fresh out! I wonder if we got rid of everything at that last tag sale we had?" she complained.

"Don't worry. There's plenty of nice statues at our church bookstore. You're welcome to shop there or if you want me to pick something up for you I could get you something next week after church," I told her.

"Oh that would be super! You're a dear."

"What kind of statue are you looking for?" I asked.

"What do you recommend?"

"I think a statue of the Blessed Mother is the best choice, but you may also want to get a statue of Saint Michael for protection. You decide."

"I think I will get a statue of Mary. Didn't Father tell you to have recourse to her? And if we're going to wear her medal and say prayers I think seeing an image of her would be most suitable. Let me know what the cost is and I'll pay you back."

"Will do," I turned to notice Ricky picking at my cake. "Hey!" I yelled, "Wait until I cut that! Joanne I have to go. I'll talk to you later."

Chapter 3

Monday morning Rick was up bright and early and left as usual for work.

"It's gonna be another hot one. Why don't you let the kids go for a swim?" he asked me as he kissed me goodbye and hurried out the door.

I decided to pull out the little kiddie pool we had on our deck for the kids to play in. Then I began to pick things up around the house and vacuum. When I finished with that I washed the breakfast dishes and put a load of laundry in the washing machine. It was getting hot outdoors and the kids were all anxious for me to fill the little pool. They cheered as I dragged the hose around back.

"Go get your bathing suits on!" I yelled to them.

They were back in no time screaming with glee. I pulled up a deck chair and put my tired hot feet into the pool as they splashed and enjoyed the cool water.

"Don't splash too much water out! I'm not going to keep filling it up all day!"

While they were having such a good time, I decided to go inside and make lunch. I took out some cold cuts from the refrigerator and grabbed a jar of mayo and a loaf of bread. As I got to work making sandwiches I turned on the TV to see the news.

"Today is August 2nd and here now is the news. Rain, rain and more rain for the entire eastern seaboard. Heavy torrential rains are expected today . . ."

I wasn't really paying any attention to it. The same stories seemed to be repeated every day. It was getting so monotonous.

I left the TV on and went to grab a few towels for the bathers before heading back outside with their sandwiches.

"All right, out of the pool!" I told them. "Dry off before you eat!"

The three of them were hungry so it didn't take much to coax them to get out. They each wrapped a fluffy big towel around their blue little bodies and waited in the warm sun for their lunch. I hurried back with their sandwiches. It was such a nice day for us. It was hard to think of so many people having troubles with flooding or drought or digging out from the earthquake in Indonesia or evacuating the Hawaiian Islands.

As I watched them happily enjoying their lunch, I looked up to the sky to watch the clouds drifting by. I remembered when I was a kid how we used to guess what animals the clouds looked like.

"Hey," I pointed to a jumbo white billowy puff, "that cloud looks like an elephant!"

The kids started to enjoy the game.

"That one looks like a giraffe!" Daniel remarked.

"Look at that one. It looks like a bird," Ricky said.

The next one was odd looking. It had what appeared to be horns and it looked frightening.

"That one's scary mommy. It looks like the devil!" Rachel shivered.

I had to agree with her but I didn't say so out loud.

"They're only clouds. Who's ready for some watermelon?" I tried to change the subject.

They all screamed out at once.

"I am!"

"I am!"

"I am!"

"Comin' right up!" I told them as I headed for the slider to the kitchen.

The TV was still on and I caught a glimpse of a breaking story as I opened the refrigerator to retrieve the watermelon. I carried the huge piece to the counter as I kept my eye on the TV. Setting the fruit down, I opened the utensil drawer to look for a sharp knife. Finding one, I closed the drawer.

The news reporter was reporting from the orient. It was the strangest thing. There were people flocking to churches and shrines of every sort. They were leaving candles and flowers as if someone of great importance had died. They were weeping, lots of them, so many of them. I wondered why they all were crying. My kids grew impatient waiting for their treat, so I disregarded the news flash and hurried with the slices of watermelon back outside.

"Let's play the cloud game again mommy!" Rachel was excited.

I smiled looking up to the sky.

"There goes a kangaroo!" I pointed to a billowy creature.

Just then the phone rang.

"You keep looking," I told them as I hurried inside.

"Hell-o?" I picked up the phone. It was Mrs. Nelson.

"Jill, I'm so glad I found you at home. My Don tripped out back of our house and hurt his ankle pretty bad. He can't get up and there's no one around to help us. Do you think you could come over and just help me get him into the house? I'll call a doctor once we get him to the couch."

"Sure Margaret. I'll be right there."

I hung up the phone and went back out to the deck to tell Daniel he was in charge until I came back. The Nelson house was only a few houses away so I knew I wouldn't be long.

"Keep an ear out for Katie, if she wakes up from her nap. I'll be back in a few minutes. You have their phone number."

Daniel smiled back at me, "Don't worry mom. Everything's under control."

"I'm gonna call next door to keep a look out for you just the same," I smiled back at him. "I'll be right back. Behave please."

I ran down the street to the Nelson house and found Margaret waiting to show me around back. Mr. Nelson was on the ground clutching his leg and grunting with pain.

"Don't move, Don. Do you think you broke it?" I asked him.

"No. I can move it a little. I think it's just a bad sprain. Help me up to the house."

"Okay. Easy now. I'll grab his left side, Margaret. You get his right. When I count three lift him up. Ready? One, two, three and up!"

Mr. Nelson was at long last on his feet and managed to get to the front of the house where there weren't any stairs. He hobbled with us into the house.

"Set him over here in the den," Margaret thought it best not to make him go upstairs to the living room.

"Just let me sit in my chair," he persuaded us.

I got him over to his easy chair and he plopped down gratefully into it.

"Oh," he let out a groan. "That was the dumbest thing I ever did."

"I'll go get an ice pack," Margaret left us alone.

"How'd it happen?" I asked curiously.

"Never mind," he was too embarrassed to talk about it and quickly changed the subject. "Jill, would you mind switching on the TV? I missed the news this morning. Anymore storms headed our way?"

"Let's see."

I went over to turn the set on. Then I added, "You know there was the craziest story on before. Let me see if I can find out something more about it again. Somewhere in the orient they were reporting about tons of people mourning. They were gathered around a church. Some were at shrines. Everyone was lighting candles and crying. I wonder who died?"

Margaret came back into the room with an ice pack.

"Here Don, let me put this on your ankle."

As soon as I saw they had the situation under control I turned to say, "I'd better get going. The kids are by themselves. Katie must be up from her nap by now."

"Thanks for all your help," Margaret said thankfully.

"Thanks Jill," Mr. Nelson echoed.

"Keep the foot up Don and let me know what the doctor says. If you need anything else Margaret, just give me a call," with that I left them and headed back home.

The kids were just finishing up eating their watermelon. The pits were everywhere since they were having a contest to see who could spit their pit the farthest.

"I won mom!" Ricky said proudly.

"Thanks for being such good kids while I was away," I praised them.

"What happened mom?" Rachel wanted to know.

"Mr. Nelson just fell, I guess. Seems he sprained his ankle pretty bad and couldn't get up on his own. He just needed a little help getting into the house. He'll be all right."

I could hear Katie stirring in her crib.

"Kate's up! Gotta get her a bottle!"

I left the children to play as I went to check on baby Kate.

Late that same day, in the afternoon, dark storm clouds started to roll in again. It seemed like we were getting rain every day for weeks! I ran to close the screened windows and told the kids they should gather up their toys and come inside. Rick telephoned from work.

"Anything exciting going on today?" he asked me.

"Not really. I got a call from Margaret Nelson today. Seems Mr. Nelson fell outside and couldn't get up. Margaret called me to give her a hand. He seems to have sprained his ankle pretty bad."

"How's he doing now?"

"I'm not sure. I'll give them a call later. It looks like we're going to have another storm. There's some thunderhead clouds rolling in and the wind is starting to pick up a little."

"Close the windows!" Rick reminded me.

"I'm already on it."

"What are you making for dinner?" he asked.

"What do you want?"

"It's too hot to cook. How about something simple like a spinach salad or a fruit salad?"

"Fruit salad sounds good to me. And we should probably use up the rest of the fruit in case we loose power again."

"All right, honey. Get the kids in and don't let them watch TV during the storm."

"Daniel turn the TV off!" I yelled out to him. "Okay honey, drive home carefully. I'll see you later."

"I love you."

"Love you too."

After I hung up the phone I told the kids to grab a few flashlights just in case we lost power. They were happy to oblige.

Meanwhile the Sullivan children were busy finishing up a game of whiffle ball. It was Patrick and Chris against Ed and Jimmy. Score was six to seven in favor of Ed's team.

"My turn!" Jimmy yelled as he got up to bat.

Edward stood ready to run as soon as Jimmy hit the ball. Just then Mrs. Sullivan came out of the house calling them to come on in before the storm was overhead. There were little rumbles of thunder in the distance. Occasional flashes of lightening could be seen.

"Come on now! You can finish up with that game later," she warned them.

"We'll be right there, ma!" Patrick didn't care about going indoors.

The pitch was in. Jimmy missed. Another ball went sailing through the air. It was beginning to get a little windy. Jimmy tipped the ball.

"Foul!" Patrick cried out.

Just then a fierce bolt of lightening ripped through the blackened sky and a loud clap of thunder echoed shortly after it. All the boys dropped everything and dashed quickly into the house!

"Wipe your feet!" Mrs. Sullivan was standing at the door as her boys came in.

The thirsty crew headed for the refrigerator to find something cool to drink. Mrs. Sullivan went to the dryer to get out the clean clothes. She called to Mary Alice and Colleen to help her fold them.

"Colleen would you and your sister please put these away. I'm going to start getting dinner ready before we loose power. Maybe I'll fire up the grill. Keep the TV off when the storm gets close," she instructed before heading to the patio to prepare the grill for cooking.

James was first to the TV so he would have first dibs on what they were all going to watch. He quickly turned to cartoons. The rest of the boys, too tired to fight with him, just came into the room and plopped down on any open seat.

Mrs. Sullivan got busy in the kitchen chopping lettuce and tomatoes for their salad. She cut and washed eight large baking potatoes and wrapped them in foil for the grill.

"Patrick will you help me husk the corn?" she called out.

Patrick came at once to do one of his favorite chores. Mrs. Sullivan took out the marinated steaks from the refrigerator and placed them on the countertop until the grill was hot enough to cook on. In the meanwhile, Patrick washed off the clean corn on the cob and placed them in a huge pot to cook over the stove.

"Is that all you need me for?" he asked his mother.

"Thanks, Pat!" she smiled at him. "You're a good one!"

He kissed her tenderly on the cheek and grabbed a slice of cucumber as he headed back to join his brothers in the family room.

Mary Alice was on the computer always sending on-line instant messages to her friends. She was chatting about the *Three Days of Darkness* when suddenly she started to receive some more startling information. A friend of hers began to tell her about the warnings at Fatima, Portugal. The Blessed Mother had appeared to three children there in 1917.

"There's a more recent warning from Our Lady given to a Sister Agnes Sasegawa in Akita, Japan on October 13, 1973!" her friend began to type in the message.

"The Blessed Mother told her, if men do not repent and better themselves, God the Father will inflict a terrible chastisement on all humanity. It will be a punishment greater than the deluge, such as one has never seen before. Fire will fall from the sky and will wipe out a great part of humanity, the good as well as the bad, sparing neither priests nor faithful. The survivors will find themselves so desolate that they will envy the dead."

Mary Alice typed back, "Where did you find this?"

"It's on the internet."

"The Blessed Mother spoke to this nun three times in 1973. The last time was on the 56th anniversary of the last apparition of Our Lady at Fatima. This new warning is an update of both the warnings and the promise of Fatima. Cardinal Ratzinger, now Pope Benedict XVI, approved this apparition in June of 1988. He said it is *reliable and worthy of belief.*

"He continues to relate that the two messages of Fatima and Akita are essentially the same. There is a very specific warning of a worldwide chastisement. A chastisement of cataclysmic proportion is about to befall the world!"
"Mary Alice dinner is ready! Turn that computer off!" Mrs. Sullivan yelled up the stairs.
"I'm coming, ma!" she logged herself off and ran downstairs to tell her mother the news.

As the Sullivans gathered around the dining room table for Grace a bolt of lightening flashed overhead and power was lost.
"Light the candles," Mrs. Sullivan ordered her boys. She had placed the matches and candles strategically on the table knowing they may need them. Just then Mr. Sullivan burst into the house, home from work!
"There's a big storm heading up the coast again today! Is this weather ever going to change?" he blurted out.
"Come and eat. Dinner is on the table," Mrs. Sullivan began to lead them in prayer.

When everyone had filled their plates Mary Alice began in earnest to tell all of them the startling news she had just heard over the internet. Knowing her mother believed everything about the *Three Days of Darkness* that were going to occur, she turned to her with a final plea, "They said this chastisement isn't far away at all now! It could happen any day!"
"There, there now," Mr. Sullivan jumped in. "Don't go rufflin' your feathers about all this."
"Let the child speak, Sean," Mrs. Sullivan turned her attention back to Mary Alice. "Go on child."
"Fire will fall from the sky! That's what Father McGrath told us too on Sunday . . ."

❧

I closed most of the windows in the house before the rain started to pour out of the sky. I was upstairs when I heard the front door burst open and Rick rushed in shaking off his wet clothes.

"I'm home! Where is everybody?" he called out.

The kids were busy playing a game, while I tried frantically to shut the last of the windows.

"I'll be right down," I called out to him.

As I came down the stairs I didn't see Rick near the front door. I didn't think anything of it, so I headed to the kitchen to cut up some fruit for the fruit salad. I hummed a little song as I worked. The storm was howling outside so I refrained from putting the TV on. I always heard it was important not to have electrical appliances going when an electrical storm is overhead.

I chopped the strawberries and washed the grapes. I sliced the cantaloupe and cut up some watermelon. There were a few peaches left, so I put them into the big bowl as well. I opened a can of chunked pineapple and drained off the juice. I added that to the salad. I topped it off with a half pint of fresh blueberries. As I tossed all the fruit together I decided we would top the meal with some sherbet. I checked the freezer to make sure we had enough. Then I looked in the breadbox for some dinner rolls and got out the butter.

I set the table with paper plates and brought the rest of the food to the table as well. I lit some candles just in case our lights went out. As I turned the corner to go get the kids I spotted Rick watching the news on TV in the living room. His eyes were wide and focused. He didn't hear me come into the room.

"Come on honey, dinner's ready. You shouldn't have that thing on during a storm," I told him.

I went looking for the kids.

"Wash your hands and come and eat!" I yelled.

I went back to the dinner table and sat down there waiting for everybody to join me. All of a sudden there was a loud sound of fighting and then all I heard was, "Mommy, mommy,

Daniel just hit me and look it's bleeding!" Ricky held out his
arm to show me where Daniel had hit him with a toy.

"Daniel!" I scolded him, "How many times have I told you
never to hit your brother?"

I turned to Ricky and noticed it wasn't a bad cut, just a
pretty good scratch that I quickly began to wash with water
and then I grabbed for a bandaid. I turned back to Daniel to
scold him again and noticed that he was bent over seemingly
in great pain. He was also crying.

"Daniel!" I ran to him overly concerned, "Daniel? What
is it?"

He didn't answer me for a few moments. He was crying
so hard he could hardly speak. His face was nearly blue at his
trying to choke out the words but slowly he managed to let
the words escape.

"I'm sorry mommy. I'm so sorry. I knew I shouldn't have
hit Ricky! I'm sorry Ricky! Please forgive me! Please! Please
forgive me!" he burst into a floodgate of tears and couldn't
be comforted.

"Daniel!" I screamed at him trying to keep him from
becoming hysterical. "It's all right. Ricky's fine! He just has a
scratch! He knows you're sorry!"

At which point Ricky fell to the floor and began to lament
with even louder wails than his brother.

"I'm so sorry mommy. It was all my fault! I started the
whole thing. I was making fun of Daniel for no reason at all.
If I had been kinder this never would have happened . . ." he
trailed off screaming and crying in a real contrite manner as
he managed to crawl across the floor to where Daniel was and
put his little arm about his brother. Anyone could see they
were both terribly sorry for their behavior.

They were both terribly sorry for their sins!

It hit me all at once! I remembered what Father McGrath
had told us, "A prodigy will occur showing every person how
they have offended Almighty God! This will be a time of

intense suffering where many people will wish to die, but no one will!"

"I want to die!" Daniel called out.

"No, I should be the one to die! Take me Lord!" Ricky cried.

A terrible feeling of doom and uncertainty began to circulate in the room. My heart broke for the both of them as I began to feel it was my fault for not being more stern with them. Perhaps I should have been a different kind of mother. I began to feel unworthy and dejected. I began to feel a great remorse, a feeling of deep and intense sorrow. Seeing their tears, I began to cry with them.

"What's going on here?" Rick entered the room demanding to know. Then he burst into tears himself seeing all of us so drained and sad.

"We have to stop! Stop it I say, at once!" he stood in the midst of us as we all looked earnestly at him for a solution.

"Remember yourselves! Don't forget that Father warned us about discouragement. It is the tool of the devil! Don't give in to it! Daniel you've apologized and so did you Ricky! Now be done with it. Go wash your faces and come back here for dinner!"

Rick picked us all up from the floor and after the children had gone he looked at me and told me to go turn on the television. I did as he told me to do and couldn't believe my eyes. The news reporter was stationed some place in the Middle East. Thousands of people were lamenting and no one could tell why. People were gathered at the great Wailing Wall in Jerusalem begging God for forgiveness, while others stood further off and struck their breasts over and over asking God to be merciful.

"Have you been watching the news today? This is going on all over the world. The prodigy has come!" Rick looked at me.

"I don't know what to say. I feel so terribly sad. I could cry for ages. There are so many things I regret that I've done in my life! Will God ever forgive me?" and I began to cry uncontrollably and remorsefully.

Rick took me in his arms, still looking over my shoulder to the television blaring. Everyone was crying. There was a deafening sound from such a multitude of sorrows.

"What have I done with my life?" Rick slowly began to break down, but he tried as best he could to hold back great tears and not frighten the children.

Chapter 4

The next morning brought little relief to the depressed state we all were in. Rick tried to be strong pushing us onward to do our best and try with all our might not to become discouraged.

"Why don't you take the kids for a ride to the church bookstore and get Joanne and John the statue you promised them?" Rick suggested. "It may change your mood, going out and doing something to help someone else."

I wiped away the tears that were rolling down my cheeks. It sounded like a good thing to do. I needed to buy her a statue. I was determined to help my friend, "Yes, I'll get the kids ready to go right after breakfast."

Rick kissed me goodbye.

"I love you," he wept. "But we have to be strong! God wants us to help one another, love one another, and by going to that bookstore today, you'll be doing what He wants."

"You're right, honey. I love you too," I kissed him back as he left for work.

The phone rang. It was Joanne. She was crying.

"I can't stop crying," she began. "John and Jess can't either. We're such a mess. We have this overwhelming feeling of deep remorse for so many things."

"Joanne!" I tried to get her attention, "The prodigy is here! It's going on everywhere, all over the world. People are sorry for having offended God. You have to be strong! You can't get discouraged! Listen, I'm going down to the church bookstore this morning. Why don't you come with me? I was going to pick a statue out for you, but why don't you pick one out for yourself?"

I waited for her reply.

She stopped her sobbing.

"The prodigy? Oh my God!" she tried to compose herself realizing the serious state our fates were in. "What time are you going?"

"Why don't you come over now? We can have a cup of coffee before we head out."

"I can be there in half an hour."

"I'll see you then."

Daniel came into the kitchen just as I hung up the phone. He was blowing his nose and wiping his face drenched with tears.

"Who was that on the phone, mommy?"

"It was Auntie Joanne. She's coming over and we're all going on an adventure today! Go and tell Ricky and Rachel to get ready."

His childlike interest sparked and his sorrow turned to wonder and joy. He did just as I told him to do. "Ricky! Rachel! We're going on an adventure!"

I turned to wipe the countertop and fill my coffee mug. I was beginning to feel a little better myself. Then I hurried upstairs to change baby Kate and get dressed before they came.

Ricky jumped down the stairs when the doorbell rang. I followed him down holding Kate in my arms. Joanne and Jess came inside. Their faces were red and drawn from hours of crying.

"Come on in! Are you ready for our adventure Jess?" I tried to spark her interest too.

She seemed to perk up at those words and seeing the boys and Rachel coming down to greet her. They all cheered at once and ran outside to play. I watched them go putting Kate down in the adjacent playpen.

"Come on," I turned to my dear friend. "Let's go have a cup of coffee."

Joanne followed me into the kitchen and sat down at the table wiping the last of her tears from her face.

"Here's a tissue," I handed her the nearby box.

"Thank you," she began. "I didn't think I'd ever stop crying. I felt so awful."

"I know, we did too. But it's everywhere! Rick was the first to make the connection. It's the prodigy. We're all supposed to feel remorse for offending God. Think of the people who don't realize what is happening."

"Journalists should be telling everyone about this prophecy!" Joanne protested.

"They'll never do that. There are so many atheists. Some people are never gonna know what hit them. I think they're going to keep this a cover up because it's too frightening a concept."

I tried to change the subject.

"Come on. Let's go get your statue. We haven't a moment to spare."

I got up and called the kids to come in from the back slider door. They came running and screaming at once.

"Everybody into the van!" I tried to smile at them. "I'll drive."

After strapping Kate into her car seat we drove off on our mission to our church.

We found the church parking lot exceptionally full that August week day. People packed the church praying their rosaries, coming early to Mass, and lighting candles. They too realized the gravity of the situation.

"Come on Jo," I motioned her to the bookstore.

Hazel was standing behind the counter wiping her face from sweat and tears. She was a very pleasant elderly lady that volunteered her time running the bookstore.

"Hell-o Jill. What can I do for you?" she tried to smile.

"Hi Hazel. It's not what you can do for me, but what you can do for my friend here. She's looking for a statue," I replied.

"Any one in particular?" she asked.

"A nice one of the Blessed Mother," Joanne interjected.

"Well you've come to the right place. We have a lovely assortment right over here."

Hazel's mood also seemed to change as she began to help us.

There was an entire shelf of statues. Some were big, others small, but all beautifully painted and ready to be purchased.

"I think I like that one!" Joanne pointed to the tall one on the top shelf.

"She is a beauty!" Hazel remarked as well, getting her down for Joanne and heading back to the cash register. "Will there be anything else?"

"Yes," I interrupted. "Would we be able to have Father bless it?"

"Father has already blessed it. In fact he blessed nearly everything in this shop. People are buying up religious articles like we were going out of business. You can't be too careful these days," she smiled at us.

"Thanks, Hazel," I smiled back at her. "God bless you."

We left the store and headed back home.

"Do you want to stay for lunch?" I asked Joanne as we drove.

"No, I think I'll head home and do a little more preparing for you know what," she gave me a wink of her eye.

"Is it all right if Jess stays awhile, please mommy, please?" Ricky asked me.

"Is it all right if Jess stays awhile?" I turned to Joanne. "They get along so nicely."

"Sure. I'll pick her up later."

I pulled into our driveway and everyone jumped out of the van. The kids ran off to play hide and seek.

"I'll call you later," Joanne proceeded to get into her car.

I got Kate out of the car seat quietly. She had fallen asleep. I hurried to put her in her crib for her nap. While she was napping I decided to go on the computer to do a little research about the prophecy of the *Three Days of Darkness*.

There were quite a few websites regarding this impending punishment. I came across one that said a miracle was going to take place in Garabandal, Spain before the chastisement. It was going to be announced eight days beforehand and a sign was going to mark it after it took place. It was going to be televised and seen around the world. But this was speculation. The Catholic Church didn't give credence to any of it.

There were also some predictions posted that had already passed without their coming true. I sat still thinking about what to do next. I began to wonder if it was all sensationalism. It seemed that nearly everyone was expecting the apocalypse to happen any day now. All I knew was that the warning showing the sins of men, a prodigy, had already taken place. The next step was to look for a miracle!

Mrs. Nelson had telephoned Maureen Sullivan to ask if one of her boys would cut their lawn since Mr. Nelson was out of commission with a fractured ankle.

"The doctor wants him off his feet for the next two months at least!" Mrs. Nelson told her.

"That's too bad," Mrs. Sullivan answered. "I'm sure I can get Patrick to oblige you. He's always looking for a few extra dollars and he's such a good boy."

"Yes, he is. And we'd be so grateful for his help. Mr. Nelson will be sure to pay him, if he can make it here every week or so."

"Patrick! Patrick!" Mrs. Sullivan called out for her son. She covered the receiver of the phone as he entered the room.

"What is it?" he asked his mother.

"Mr. Nelson fractured his ankle and they need someone to cut their lawn for the next couple of weeks. They said they'd pay you. Please say you'll help them out. They're our neighbors and I'm sure they would help us out too if we were in need."

Patrick was a good soul responding quickly, "Sure I'll do it for them, ma. When do they need me over there?"

"When do you need him to start?" Maureen spoke back into the phone.

"He'll do it? Oh, that's wonderful!" Mrs. Nelson covered her receiver. "When do you want him to start, Don?"

Mr. Nelson was reading the newspaper. He looked up.

"Have him stop by today. With all that rain we've been having everything is growing out of control. If he comes by at least once a week we should keep things in check."

"Can he start today Maureen? Mr. Nelson thinks it would be a good idea for Patrick to stop by here once a week. The rain has caused things to get a bit out of control. How about today?"

"Can you go over there now?" Maureen asked her son.

"Sure ma," Patrick winked at her. "I'll get right on it."

With that Patrick grabbed an apple from the fruit basket on the table and ran out the front door heading over to the Nelson house.

"He's on his way Margaret. Is there anything else we can do for you? It's going to be hard not having Don up and about. You just let me know if you need anything, all right?"

"Thanks Maureen. You're a good neighbor. I don't know what we'd do if it weren't for good folks like you."

And they continued their conversations for a short time thereafter.

Kate started to stir in her crib and I turned off the computer to change her and retrieve a bottle. The kids were all still running around outside. No sooner had I come downstairs to put Kate in her playpen then the front door opened and they were all standing there waiting for a cool drink.

"How about some refreshing lemonade?" I asked them.

They all cheered in favor of it.

"Go wash up and you can have some at the table," I instructed them as I headed to the kitchen to get cups and the pitcher of lemonade in the refrigerator. I still had some blueberry coffee cake too. "Does anybody want cake with their drink?" I shouted out.

"I'll have a piece, please," I heard Rachel shout back.

"Can we have slushies instead?" Ricky yelled.

I hadn't thought of that, but since it was so hot, slushies seemed like a good idea.

"Do you want lemon or fruit punch slushies?" I asked them.

One by one they filed into the kitchen. It was unanimous. Everyone wanted fruit punch slushies. I had some help getting the ice cubes out of their trays and dumping them into the slushie maker. Everyone watched as it chewed up the ice cubes and mixed thoroughly with the punch. It was ready to pour.

As each one took their turn filling up their cup, I cut a few slices of cake.

"Thank you for the slushie and the cake," Jess spoke so politely.

"Anytime," I smiled back at her.

Then I turned on the news to see if there were any further developments regarding the prodigy. No one was reporting anything more about it. Seems this phenomenon had subsided and things were beginning to get back to normal. At least that was what the reporter said until he mentioned news of a hurricane about to pound the southern states.

"There's a chance this one will take a turn north and head up the coastline."

"Great!" I shouted sarcastically out loud.

"What's happening?" Daniel heard me.

"Oh nothing," I didn't want to upset them. "Just more bad weather on the way," I let it go at that.

Rick had gotten off from work a little early that day. I think he was concerned about how everyone was faring after our crying spells. We were all doing fine when he came in with a big kiss and a surprise bouquet of flowers.

"Who are these for?" I questioned him playfully.

"My beautiful wife!" was his speedy reply. "How did things go today?"

"As good as can be expected."

The kids all got up from the table to go play video games, leaving Rick and I the opportunity to discuss more grownup matters.

"Did you get down to church today?" he asked me.

"Yes, we did. Joanne is now the proud owner of a blessed statue of the Blessed Mother. Hazel was working the store. She was crying as well when we arrived. The church parking lot was pretty crowded too for a weekday. Lots of people were at morning Mass. Hazel said Father blessed nearly everything in the store. People are buying up all kinds of religious articles. All the candles were lit in church too. I guess lots of people are making special offerings."

As I filled Rick in on all the details he focused his sights on the television.

"Winds are estimated at about 132 miles per hour . . ." they reported.

"Great!" Rick responded sarcastically. "A hurricane! Just what we need right now."

"Maybe we should stock up on a few things," I suggested.

"We're already stocked with enough food downstairs. Maybe I'll pick up a few gallons of bottled water. We can probably use some batteries for the flashlights. Can you think of anything else?"

"I just need some bread. Other than that I think we're ready for it. Let's not worry about all that right now. What do you want for dinner?"

"Let's have something simple. Don't heat up the kitchen."

"Do you want to have hamburgers and hot dogs? I can fire up the grill."

"That sounds great."

The phone rang. Joanne wanted Jess to come home for dinner.

"I'll drop her off," Rick volunteered looking at me, "and I'll stop by the store to get the water and batteries."

"Rick will drop her off. He has to pick up a few things at the store," I told my friend.

Joanne was happy about that. "Looks like another storm heading our way!"

"Have you seen the news? There's a hurricane about to pound the coastline!" I informed her.

"No, I was talking about the thunderstorm heading our way right now. Look outside. I better go shut all my windows. See you later," she said.

"Don't forget about the bread!" I called to Rick who was heading for the front door.

I called out for Jess, "It's time for you to go home now Jess." Everyone gathered to see her off.

"I'll be back in a little while," Rick yelled back.

"Thanks for having me," Jess smiled back too.

The sky looked overcast again. I dreaded another storm. We had been having storms for weeks. There didn't seem to be an end in sight.

"Daniel go outside and bring in all the bikes and toys. We're going to have another storm. I'm going to try and cook a few hot dogs and hamburgers before it rains." The kids ran out in all the excitement as I hurried to get busy with dinner.

⁂

"Thank you, Mr. Nelson," Patrick said as he took the money offered to him for cutting their lawn.

"You did a super job!" Mr. Nelson was pleased. "Can you come back next week the same time? It will probably be overgrown by then too."

"I'll come whenever you like. If it looks like you want me sooner or later just call," Patrick replied.

"You're a good boy!" Mrs. Nelson interjected.

Patrick blushed as he headed for the door. "Hope your ankle heals up pretty soon, Mr. Nelson," and with that he headed back home.

Mrs. Nelson turned to her husband asking what he would like for dinner.

"Why don't we finish up that shepherd's pie?" he suggested.

"How about a nice tossed salad to go with it?" Mrs. Nelson asked him as she glanced out the open window. "Oh, no!" she saw the thunderclouds rolling in again, "not another storm!"

Mr. Nelson turned to have a look, "Is it ever going to stop raining?"

"I'll turn on the TV for you, dear." then she headed off to the kitchen to prepare their meal.

Mr. Nelson tuned in just in time to see the last report of the hurricane out in the Atlantic. It was heading dead ahead for Florida and the eastern coast.

"Are there going to be anymore catastrophes?" he called out to Margaret.

"What's that, dear?" she came back into the living room.

"I said, are there going to be anymore catastrophes? There's a big hurricane heading up the coastline!"

Margaret looked out the window again, "When is it due here?"

Just as she spoke they both heard a distant rumble of thunder.

"I better shut the windows upstairs," she left her husband to watch the rest of the news, as she scrambled to close up the house yet another time.

Mr. Nelson had seen enough. He switched the channel, surfing for something of more interest. Then he found it. A baseball game was on!

⟨⟩

Rick got back just in the nick of time.

"I got everything at the store," he closed the door quickly behind him. Rain drops were just beginning to fall as I scooped up the last of the hot dogs and hamburgs from the grill. I ran back into the kitchen with them, closing the slider door abruptly behind me.

"Come and get it!" I yelled out to everyone.

The kids all hurried to the table.

"Daniel, would you please get the ketchup and mustard?" I asked for a little help, as I grabbed some potato salad and cole slaw.

Ricky was pushing Rachel's chair.

"Stop it!" Rick scolded them. "Let's say Grace. I'm starved. Let's eat!"

We all gathered around our table and bowed our heads in prayer. It was such a simple little meal, but we were all together, so safe, so thankful for what we had. Thunder broke the stillness and I jumped up to grab a couple of candles and some matches.

"Better keep these on hand, just in case," I tossed them to Rick. "I'm going to check the windows upstairs."

Taking two steps at a time I hurried up the stairs to close the open windows. Rain was just starting to pour in on the windows facing the front of the house. A bolt of lightening zapped through the air and we lost power again. Luckily it wasn't that dark out yet, so I made my way back to the kitchen without too much difficulty. I found Rick lighting the candles I left him. The children were a little frightened.

"Now isn't this cozy?" I remarked looking at a candlelit dinner table.

"I'm scared mommy," Ricky confessed.

"There, there. Nothing to worry about," Rick began. "We're all safe and sound. We're all together."

I looked over to Rick and smiled at each of our children to show I was in complete agreement.

"Poor Mr. King. Maureen Sullivan told me their cellar is already flooded. He's been pumping and bailing out the downstairs for days. I wonder if he'll ever get the chance to see it dry."

"Not with all this rain we've been having. Wonder if his house will still be standing after that hurricane heads up this way," Rick didn't have a chance to finish his thought.

"Hurricane?" Daniel shouted. "Is it a hurricane outside?"

"No, they're just predicting one to head up this way. Don't worry by the time it gets here it won't be as strong as it is right now. Those things usually just bring a lot of rain when they reach us," I interjected.

"So there's nothing to worry about," Rick jumped in. "Now eat your hamburger."

"How was your day, dear?" I looked across the table to my husband.

He smiled back, "I guess it went all right. I was thinking about what Father McGrath had said all day. It was such an odd thing, so many people upset like that all over the world. And now things are just the way they've always been. Nothing has really changed, except I think a few people might have noticed what took place." He didn't want to say anymore about it, since the children were all looking at him and they were already very scared.

"I did a little research over the internet today," I began.

Then I stopped myself from telling him what I found out about the *Three Days of Darkness*.

"Jess had a good time here today too, didn't she kids?" I asked everyone at the table.

They all seemed to cheer up a bit hearing the conversation lighten up.

"Do you think this storm will go all night, mommy?" Rachel asked.

"I'm not sure, honey. We'll keep watching the weather forecast."

A bright light flashed and a great rumble of thunder filled the house.

"That was a close one!" Rick remarked.

"Can we sleep in your bed?" Ricky asked.

"Let's see how long the storm lasts."

Chapter 5

We decided to camp out in the living room making tents out of quilts and blankets. The storm was pretty strong knocking down more tree limbs in the area and causing havoc with power lines. Then it moved off the coast out into the open sea. The hurricane seemed to follow that storm, changing its course and heading out to sea as well.

The next few days looked promising with nothing but sun and rising temperatures. There were warnings of isolated thunderstorms in the area. But the warm summer weather helped us all forget about the *Three Days of Darkness* for a while. Rick was finally on vacation for the next couple of weeks and we took advantage of the nice weather by driving to the beach to relax in the sun.

"Here we are!" Rick put the blanket down in the sand and unfolded the chairs.

The kids got busy right away making sandcastles and going for a swim. I put on my straw hat and some sunscreen before I turned on our radio to listen to some oldies. They were playing an old favorite of mine when suddenly there was a breaking news story.

"Good afternoon. Today is August 8th . . . ," then the broadcast broke up with crackling sounds and lots of static, ". . . and we have a special report. We take you to . . . Spain where a young seer . . . prepared some very . . . startling information . . ."

The radio seemed to fade out. Then it just had static noises coming out of it.

"Great, they just had a breaking news story!" I slammed the thing. "It's just our luck!"

"What are you worrying about? We're at the beach. Enjoy yourself! We can tune in to the worries of the world when we're leaving. You can listen in the car, or better still, watch it on TV when we get home," Rick tried to play it down. "Come on, we're at the beach. Relax. Pass me a cold soda, please."

I put the radio back down on the blanket listening to what Rick had said. "What kind of soda do you want?" I reached into the cooler. "There's orange, grape, or root beer."

"Pass me a root beer," he grinned.

The children were all playing happily nearby us and people everywhere around us looked undisturbed and were enjoying themselves. I stopped my fussing and laid back down on the blanket ready for a nap. I must have dozed off before I realized Rick was shaking me to wake up.

"There's another storm rolling in. We better start packing up to go," he said.

I sat up trying to get my bearings and noticed the dark clouds rolling in.

"Daniel! Ricky! Rachel! Come on we have to go now!" I called out for them.

"Look at the shells I found!" Rachel came running over to the blanket all excited.

"They're beautiful, honey. But start packing up your pails and shovels. We have to go."

We got everything loaded into the van in record time and showered off some of the sand before getting into the car for the drive home. I put on the radio to listen to some music. I forgot about the special news report. In any event, there was no further mention of it. Lightening started to flare up in the distance.

"I hope we make it home before the storm hits!" I mentioned to Rick.

"We should be all right," he assured me.

The radio was really beginning to pick up static and disturbances from the storm. It got so disrupted that I finally just turned it off. We drove home the rest of the way in silence. When we pulled into the driveway the storm was right on our tails. We quickly got out of the car and ran for the front door. Everyone made it inside the house just as another clap of thunder echoed overhead.

"That was a close one!" Daniel remarked, "I'll go get the flashlights."

It was almost routine now, preparing for the storms that seemed to hit us every day.

"I'm going to start making dinner," I headed for the kitchen.

"Why don't we just have pizza tonight? Wait until this thing passes. I'll go out in a little while," Rick suggested.

Ed King was cussing and cursing at still another storm. His cellar was a mess with at least five or six inches of water. All the pumping he did seemed to be in vain. Every day there was another storm pouring water back into the already over saturated ground. Even though Mr. Sullivan had been of great assistance helping him bail out, they just couldn't seem to stay ahead of the storms.

Mr. King yelled to his wife Susan, "I think these pumps are just about exhausted! If we get one more storm I think they'll blow!"

They were old pumps that had seen better days. There was nothing more they could do. Susan was at a loss too. She had sopped some of the water up with mops and towels, but their efforts were useless having new amounts of water pouring in near daily.

"Leave it for a while," she called down to her husband. "There's another storm brewing now!"

You could hear him curse about it. Just then the telephone rang. It was Maureen Sullivan.

"Hello Maureen," Susan picked up the phone.

"How's the cellar holding out?" Maureen asked her.

"Ed's cursing down there. We can't seem to get on top of the situation. We just keep getting more water all the time with every new storm! It's beginning to wear us out. I could just cry all over again."

She was referring to her crying spell just a few days earlier during the prodigy.

"Well, that seems to be the least of your worries, I'm calling to see if you've been watching the news. There's a very interesting story breaking in Europe. It's amazing. Have you seen it?"

"No, I've been helping Ed. I haven't had the chance to watch anything. And it's time to start dinner now. I hope I can cook something before we loose power again."

"Well, if you get a moment, turn on your set. It's really something to see. A young seer is announcing something about a miracle that is going to take place in eight days! It's supposed to be pretty spectacular."

Susan didn't take the three days warning seriously nor anything related to it. They had more pressing problems to think about. If they didn't get that water out of the basement soon they would probably have structural damage. The house was beginning to smell musty too.

"I'll give a look later." The wind outside began to pick up. "Here we go again!" Susan shouted out to her husband and told Maureen she had to go.

◎◯◎

"Can I get you anything else?" Margaret asked her husband as she placed a pillow under his elevated ankle.

Mr. Nelson was reading the newspaper. They had just finished dinner and were sitting down to relax in the living room. Margaret had just finished washing the last of the dishes and asked her husband if he'd like his dessert in the living room.

"Maybe I will have a little dish of ice cream," he mentioned.

"All right, dear," she walked back to the kitchen to fix their treats.

The house was still, except for the wind howling. They had left the TV off because of the electrical storm. It was nice having it quiet for the most part. She returned to the living room with two bowls of ice cream and after giving one bowl to her husband sat down near him on the couch.

"Does your ankle feel any better?" she asked him as they ate.

"It's starting to feel a little better, but I still have a nagging pain."

"Well, just rest, dear. Isn't it nice of that Sullivan boy to help us out with the lawn? He's such a nice boy. Maybe we should have him come by a couple of times a week, especially if these storms keep coming. I've never seen everybody's lawn look so green."

"Maybe you're right. Maybe we should have Patrick over twice a week. Don't call them now. Wait until the storm passes. See if he'd like cutting the grass two times a week," Don echoed.

They sat quietly listening to the rumbles of thunder until it sounded like there was some relief.

"Sounds like a break in the storm," Margaret said as she gathered the empty bowls to bring them to the kitchen sink.

"Margaret, would you turn on the TV please? Maybe we can catch the weather or the news."

"I'll be right back," she agreed.

Coming back into the living room Margaret approached the television and turned it on. There was some static coming over it, probably from the storm still passing overhead outside. She began turning the channels to see if there were any weather reports on. It seemed like every channel had a commercial going on it. Advertisements were in demand and they played them one after the other for what seemed like ages.

"Here's something," she finally stopped switching the channels.

"Let's just watch this," Mr. Nelson laid his paper aside and asked his wife to turn up the volume a little.

The news anchor was speaking about the war going on in the Middle East. He seemed hopeful that the soldiers would be coming home soon. Next he talked about local flooding and the weather patterns that seemed stagnate all over the globe. There were droughts in the midwest, hurricanes to the southeast, and tornados on the plains. People were still feeling tremors from the aftermath of the horrid earthquake in Indonesia.

Then he suddenly stopped his reports and turned to a nearby screen to show a picture being televised from Spain. It was a picture of a young seer eager to inform people all around the globe that in eight days a miracle would take place in the very spot from which they were reporting. Then the reporter switched quickly back to more local news and sports.

"It looks like it's letting up a little, at least for the moment," Rick looked out the picture window. "I'll go get us a pizza."

I asked the kids what they wanted on their pizza as I ran upstairs to check on Kate. She was playing with her teddy bear in her crib.

"Just get pepperoni and cheese!" I yelled down.

"Be back in a flash!" Rick called out as he closed the front door behind him.

For the next few moments I decided to tidy up a little and told the kids to leave their wet swimsuits in the hamper. They all took quick showers to get the rest of the sand off of their sunburned bodies too. I picked up the last of the scattered toys and headed downstairs to the kitchen.

There was a brief moment to watch the news. I turned on the set in time to hear the ending of the breaking story about the seer in Spain. All I could catch was the fact that this seer was predicting a miracle to occur in eight days from the very spot from which they stood.

Just then Rick was banging at the front door with the pizza. I hurried to let him in and called out to the kids to come for dinner. Everyone was pretty hungry. All that sea air really worked up our appetites.

"There's a seer in Spain predicting a miracle that is supposed to happen in eight days," I told Rick after the kids left the dinner table.

A miracle?" Rick was taken aback by such a report. Then he looked at the calendar. "Eight days from now is August 15th."

I sat stunned for a moment. I don't know if it was the way he said it or that date was just stuck in my mind. Either way, I remembered what Joanne had told me. I froze in my place looking at Rick.

"August 15th is the feast day of Saint Tarcisius, a young martyr of the Holy Eucharist!" I whispered out loud! "That's part of the warning Father McGrath told us about. It's part of the impending signs. He said there would be a miracle announced eight days before the *Three Days of Darkness* and that people will see it all over the world."

"I wonder what it could be," Rick looked back at me.

"I don't know," I answered him. "But a sign is supposed to remain that people will not be able to touch. The last of the impending signs will be a Cross in the sky. I have to call Joanne!"

No sooner had I said those words than the telephone rang. Joanne was on the same wave length as me. She too had just witnessed the news and heard all about the seer's predictions.

"Next week is the feast day of Saint Tarcisius," she mentioned. "Things are falling right into place."

"Just be on guard now. We have to stand ready. Tell as many people as you can that there's a punishment on the way! Maybe we can hang posters in the stores. How are we going to get this information out?"

"And what about those who aren't going to believe us anyway?"

To which I replied, "Heaven help them!"

⚬

The next week was frantic as we tried our best to inform as many people as we could about the impending events that seemed imminent to happen. We sat in front of the supermarkets with huge signs. We had rosary beads to give away for free. Father McGrath gave us little vials of holy water. But we didn't seem to get our message across. People laughed at us. People sneered. People passed by us not stopping to even notice what we had to offer them.

"Everybody has been saying it's the end of the world for centuries! What makes you think it's going to happen in a couple of days?" one old man chuckled at us.

"This is a prophecy. It's not the end of the world. It's a punishment. Take a rosary, please. There's no time to loose. It can't hurt to be prepared," I implored him.

He could see the seriousness in my expression. He took the beads, but I knew he would only carry them away with him. He would never say the prayers attached to them.

"What a waste of time!" Joanne finally threw her arms in the air.

"It's not a waste. If we save only one soul it will be worth our while," I responded sadly. "Maybe when they see the miracle on August 15th they'll remember what we told them and put two and two together."

So we stayed there in front of the store, day after day, trying to convey our thoughts and hoping we would help at least a few people. But because our efforts were so unrewarded, we didn't go back to the store the day of the miracle. August 15th we stayed at home. We were hoping to see the miracle for ourselves on TV.

I invited Joanne over to have coffee with me that morning. She brought Jess and John too. The children were glad to be together. It helped having them all go out to play while the grownups got the chance to talk. Rick was still on vacation and John had taken the day off to see what was going to happen. We all gathered around the kitchen table as I turned on the little TV on the countertop and brought a pot of coffee over to serve everyone.

It was a peaceful day, not much happening anywhere in the world. Nothing of any significance was being broadcasted. Even the weather was unremarkable. We went over our plans and what we would do should the bitter cold night come upon us. Joanne had finished preparing her family room moving a huge piece of plywood behind the drapes that she planned to move and nail over the slider doors. She didn't want to take any chances being tempted to look out.

"I think we're ready too," I replied. "I put a few folding chairs in the laundry room so we won't have to sit on the floor. I also left enough space so we can prostrate when we pray. Did you remember to put a manual can opener in your room? No electrical things are going to work."

"Yeah," John responded. "If this thing really happens it's gonna be pretty creepy."

"Don't say *if*. It *is* going to happen! We're being warned. Time is running out. The obvious has already happened. We're going to be chastised and we need to be brave and pray!"

Rick was starting to come around, believing more and more that something was about to take place, even though he had been such a skeptic before.

"What if it strikes at night? How will we know it's the beginning of the three dreaded days?"

"First it's going to be a *bitter cold* night. Second there isn't going to be any light. If you see the stars and the moon disappearing you will know that the time is at hand. If it happens during the day, after a bitter cold night, the sky will become as ink and people will realize something very wrong is about to occur."

We continued our conversations reasoning and preparing for what lay ahead.

⟡

Meanwhile, Mr. Nelson was trying to hop around to get the newspaper. He had grown tired of sitting all day in a chair.

"Don!" Mrs. Nelson yelled seeing him up. "You know you're supposed to sit in that chair. What if you fall again? Then what? Now get back in your chair and behave. You have to listen to doctor's orders!"

Almost falling at hearing his wife shout, Don turned about and headed for his chair. Just before he reached the chair he twisted the same ankle again. He let out a terrible cry!

"Don!" Margaret came running to his rescue. "Don, are you all right?"

He cursed a few times, at his own stupidity. Then he grabbed at his leg and asked Margaret to fetch him a cold pack. She immediately headed to the kitchen for some ice.

"Now you really have no choice! You'll have to stay in that chair no matter what!" she gave him the ice pack.

Mary Alice Sullivan was back on her computer instant messaging her friends. Everyone was abuzz with the news of the three days approaching. She quickly typed in that a miracle was going to take place that very same day and would be seen all over the world. Her friend responded by signing off and telling her she was going to go watch for it on her TV.

The television was already on in the Sullivan house. Everyone was waiting to see what was going to happen. Mrs. Sullivan phoned the King household to tell them to tune in. Telephones all over the neighborhood were abuzz with curiosity and concern.

"It's time to take action," Mrs. Sullivan warned her friend Susan. "If you haven't yet prepared a room you should do so now! The seer already gave the warning that a miracle was going to take place today. Father McGrath warned us about this too. It's going to be seen all over the world. Do you have a blessed candle?"

"I think we have one somewhere around here. We've been so preoccupied with the water in the cellar there's been little or no time to do anything else," Susan answered her.

"I can give you one if you need it. How about holy water? Do you have any on hand?"

"Now really Maureen, don't you think you're over reacting just a little too much?" Susan laughed at her.

"It's true I tell you. Please Susan, you have to listen to me! Your very life depends on it!"

Maureen could hear Ed yelling in the background.

"I have to go, sweetie. The boss is raving! Don't worry about us. We'll be all right. At least we haven't had anymore rain today! That's a plus," and with that she hung up.

Maureen put down her receiver slowly. She was worried her friend didn't take her warnings seriously. She quickly pulled her rosaries out of her pocket and began to pray. Then she hurried off to finish another load of laundry.

"Chris, would you and Mary Alice make the beds for me please?" she called out. "And Colleen would you please get lunch started?"

Everyone was busy as the TV blared in the background.

☙❧

Meanwhile back at our house, I asked Joanne if they'd like to stay for lunch. Nothing was happening on the TV. I turned the volume way down low so we could continue our conversations.

"Do you need any help?" she volunteered to make sandwiches.

"No, well maybe. Would you ask everybody what they'd like? I have ham and cheese, bologna, or peanut butter and jelly," I told her.

Joanne called outside for the kids to come in and wash up. Then she took their orders as they filed in. I quickly made the children a little picnic lunch setting up paper plates on the table out on the deck. They were happy to eat outside. The grownups kept inside in the kitchen.

"What do you make of all this, John?" Rick asked him.

"Well, I was a skeptic at first. But after all these other things starting to happen, I've changed my mind. I think there is something to these warnings after all. I just can't imagine what the real chastisement is going to be like."

"Would anyone like a little fruit salad?" I asked.

"That sounds so refreshing, especially on a hot day like this!" John and Joanne both agreed.

"I was a skeptic too, but it is starting to get a little unnerving," Rick added. Then he turned to me and asked, "Is there anything on the TV yet?"

I cast a quick look on the tube.

"Nothing but commercials playing. Let's eat. It will probably be on when we least expect it."

"You're probably right, Jill. What's that saying? A watched pot never boils?"

We ate our lunch discussing what we would do when the actual time was at hand for the catastrophes to occur. Then Joanne helped me clear the table for some dessert and tea. The kids finished up their sandwiches and wanted some popsicles.

I put the kettle on and went into the dining room to get my china tea cups. I had some pineapple banana cream cake ready to be served with the tea. As I put everything out ready to be served, I glanced quickly at the TV to see if I was missing anything.

Lo and behold, something was happening. Something I had never seen before. It was mesmerizing, so much so that I stopped in my tracks and didn't say a word. Rick noticed me standing there staring at the television set and jumped up at once to join me.

"What is it? Is the miracle happening? Is there something taking place? What the . . . ?" he too froze nearby me.

Joanne and John jumped up at once.

"What the . . . ?" John whispered outright.

I couldn't believe my eyes. Not one of us could believe what we were seeing.

Chapter 6

The second of the impending signs had come. A sign was left to remind us that it had come. News reporters all over the world kept flashing back to the sight in Spain to view the phenomenon that stayed behind as a permanent sign. Shock and disbelief filled most of the skeptics. But acknowledgement and real concern filled those who knew what was going to take place next.

We still couldn't believe our eyes. It seemed so surreal. We couldn't yet fathom that a real prophecy was unfolding right before us. We knew from this warning the punishment was not far off. And yet it took a few days for it to really sink in.

Father McGrath was exceptionally precise when he spoke to us from the pulpit that Sunday. He was a little shaken too from what he had seen.

"There's no turning back. We're in full swing of a punishment about to take place at any time now! You can't say that you weren't warned beforehand. Everything that has been foretold has come to light. We're heading for the biggest scourge mankind has ever seen. Prepare yourselves before it's too late! Make sure you have blessed candles and holy water in your homes. I'll be in the confessional for anyone who needs me after Mass. You can't take anymore chances."

"For those of you who haven't followed along, let me give you a quick review. This prophecy has been circulating in the church since the 1800's. Many seers from very different parts of the world spoke about it. This chastisement is going to be severe because of man's offending the Almighty God. It will not be the end of the world, but will seem like it is in its severity. Three quarters of the human race will be annihilated. Hurricanes of fire will pour out of Heaven and spread all over the earth. Many will perish. Hell will be emptied and the demons will set forth over all the earth doing harm in whatever ways they can. Pestilence and poisonous gases will fill the air. Many will die of fear!"

"We have been warned! These seers told us that a prodigy would come. And didn't we all feel that sense of remorse? Didn't we all have that good cry? This part of the prophecy has already come true and passed. And then a seer predicted a miracle was going to take place on the feast day of a young martyr of the Holy Eucharist. Look at what was shown to the world from Spain! Can we really believe our eyes? Yes, we must believe! Let the skeptics pass by wondering what all this means. So much the worse for them. When this punishment hits full force they will have no time to reconsider their obstinacies."

"Prepare yourselves a room, a place in your homes, in which to take shelter and pray! When you perceive a bitterly cold night go inside and lock all your doors and windows. Stay away from the doors and windows! Don't look out! Don't talk to anyone outside! Pull the shades down and cover the windows.

You will not be permitted to see the wrath of God! Anyone who looks or goes outside will die immediately!"

"Light your blessed candles. Nothing will put them out once they are lit in the houses of those who are believers. These candles will not burn in the houses of scoffers and unbelievers. Woe to them who will be left in the dark! If you haven't already obtained a good supply of holy water, get some after Mass. Sprinkle this everywhere in your homes, especially on the doors and windows. The demons do not like holy water. It burns them!"

"Stock up on nonperishable food items such as canned goods and the like. Your utilities will not work! You won't be able to cook, nor have use of any electric lights or appliances. Keep plenty of drinking water and blankets on hand."

"Once you have established your room of refuge, pray! Pray a great deal! Pray like you have never prayed before! Pray with outstretched hands. Pray prostrate! Pray for many souls to be saved! Pray and read. Read spiritual books. Constantly pray and constantly read! There will be no time to spare. The demons will be relentless in their efforts to engulf mankind. You must be just as earnest to withstand them!"

"Anoint your eyes, ears, nose and mouth with holy water. Pray God you do not sin by your senses! Pray the rosary. Meditate on the passion of our Lord. Call upon the Blessed Mother for assistance, St. Joseph and Saint Michael the Archangel. Use ejaculations such as, *'Who is like unto God?'* Cling to your holy faith and trust in God's mercy. No one will escape the terror of these days!"

Then Father McGrath did something I have never seen a priest do before. All of a sudden he broke down and began to weep. He had done everything he could to forewarn us and now he was leaving us to survive this ordeal on our own. I think it finally was beginning to sink in with all of us, the severity of this matter. And I think the poor man inundated with phone calls and blessing people's houses and blessing statues and making gallons of holy water, was worn out. He tried to look over the church, at his parishioners, for what seemed like the last time. He realized he would not see all of us together there again. Some weren't going to survive this terrible ordeal. Some were going to die of fright. Some were going to be disobedient to the warnings. Some were scoffers and would believe too late. Some might be traveling and would die on the road home. Some would not make it to a secure place.

In all the confusion some would keep a level head and make it to a well prepared spot. They would pray with outstretched arms and do all that was instructed for them to do. These would be the faithful who would survive it. He seemed to wonder who if any he would ever see again.

He tried to compose himself, pulling out a handkerchief and blowing his nose.

"Forgive me," he tried to begin again. "I've never been called to protect my sheep to such an extent before." He realized how much he loved all of us, "I want the best for each of you. I pray God will be merciful and spare you all much hardship. I beg you to remember what I have tried to tell you here these past weeks. It's for your own good. Remember the promise that once these days have passed there will be a new world. People will be more spiritual and renewed. The world as we have known it will be changed. God isn't doing this because of hatred. He is doing this because He loves us. He wants us to get back on track and bound for Heaven. He wants us to turn from evil and come back to what is good. The world has turned its back on God for such a long time now. People have gone their merry ways sinning for so long."

"It's time for a change. It's time to face the punishment that lies just ahead. We've been asking for it. We've been provoking God. We are in need of His cleansing wrath. Remember my words to you. You have been warned. I think most of you are prepared."

Next he held up his rosary beads to all of us and ended with, "Here is the weapon that will do you the most protection. Use them! Pray the rosary! May God bless and keep all of you."

Then he turned off his microphone and headed back to the altar to recite the Credo.

We were all quiet on the ride home from church that Sunday. The children knew things were quite serious having seen the miracle on TV and seeing Father cry. Rick was deep in thought and I just couldn't bring myself to say anything further. I too was wondering who would survive this ordeal. I wondered if Rick would come through it with our children. I wondered if I would be brave enough. I wondered if I'd ever see Father McGrath again or our church. I wondered if our church would be torn to pieces in the wake of the wrath of Almighty God. I wondered if the neighborhood would ever look the same after the chastisement.

Would we still have our neighbors? Would they survive the trials? What was the earth going to really be like? Would there be dead bodies strewn all over, putrid and rotting in the streets? Who would help to bury the dead? Or would there be a miraculous earth awaiting the survivors with lush farmlands and flowers like those in the Garden of Eden?

We pulled into the driveway of our house. I looked it all over with a deeper appreciation than I had ever felt before. I looked at the trees and the gardens of flowers. I took it all in hoping it would stay that way forever in my mind.

I unstrapped Kate from her car seat and brought her into the house for a nap. The children followed me in, rather solemnly. Rick came in last turning the TV back on to see if there was anymore breaking news.

Mr. Sullivan and his oldest son Chris were busy nailing plywood to the family room windows. Mr. Sullivan was in earnest now getting ready for the prophecy to come true. Mrs. Sullivan was busy cooking Sunday dinner. She wasn't sure if it would be their last cooked meal for some time. Colleen helped peel some potatoes while Patrick read to the younger children to keep them preoccupied. Mary Alice was on the computer.

"Maybe I should call Susan and see if they have a room prepared?" Mrs. Sullivan walked over to her husband looking at his work.

"They're not buying any of this. They've been so concerned about the water in their basement that they hardly care about anything else," Mr. Sullivan replied.

"But maybe one last try will work!" Maureen was so hopeful.

"Go ahead then, if it will make you feel better. Why don't you go over there?" he smiled at her.

Maureen took out a blessed candle and headed over to her neighbor's house. All the while she thought about what she was going to say when she got there. This might be her last chance to convince them they had better take her seriously. She was eager as she rang the doorbell. She waited. She rang it again. No one answered.

"I guess no one is home," she finally remarked. But she couldn't leave there not having delivered her blessed candle. She placed it very conspicuously on the front stoop and walked away. She knew they'd be sure to find it.

It was no different at the Nelson house. They too were getting ready. Margaret was busy checking the shades on the windows and looking over their drapes. She was certain the windows would be covered completely and there wouldn't be even the slightest chance to peek out. She wanted to be very certain of that. Don just sat quietly reading the paper. He accepted the fact that he had to keep his leg elevated or suffer with problems further down the line. He trusted his wife to be quite able to make all the preparations necessary to survive three long days of darkness. He looked up to notice her putting out a couple of blessed candles. One went on the table near the picture window in the den, while the other went on an end table in the same room. She placed a jug of holy water near the later candle and positioned a box of matches near there too.

"Would you like a sandwich, Don?" she finally looked over to him.

"No thanks. But I would like a piece of fruit. What do we have?"

Margaret went to the kitchen at once to have a look in the refrigerator, "We have plums and peaches." She pushed aside some leftovers and found more fruit, "We also have some cherries and strawberries."

"The cherries sound good. I'll have some of them," he called out to her.

He listened as she washed some of them off in the sink and looked in the cabinet for a bowl. Then she came back to join her husband who was in their living room. She picked up a book and began to read it.

As she was reading she suddenly let out a little gasp thinking about her neighbor Mr. Enrich. She wondered if he had taken her seriously and if his blessed candle was handy. Don looked over at her.

"Are you all right?" he asked.

"It's nothing, Don. I was just thinking about Dave. I hope he's getting ready. Do you think I should call him?"

"He'll be all right. You gave him that candle. I'm sure he'll be fine."

So they left things like that. Margaret picked her book back up and Mr. Nelson turned back to reading the newspaper.

Meanwhile back at our house, the children were busy playing video games while Rick and I sat together in the living room. I had just finished washing all the dinner dishes and it was time for a little rest. Rick turned off the TV and put his arm around me pulling me closer to him on the couch.

"Do you think we'll all come through this?" I asked him beginning to doubt our endurances.

"I think we're gonna be just fine," he tried to reassure me.

"What about the baby? What are we going to do with Kate?" I was concerned.

"I don't know," Rick hadn't really thought about Kate, but he knew he would protect her in spite of whatever happened.

"I think it's going to be rough on the boys. I wonder about Rachel. She's so sensitive."

"Don't give up on us now!" Rick tried to encourage me. "We need you to be strong. The kids will feel safe if we hold things together. We know what we have to do. When the time comes we'll just do it."

"You're right. We have to be strong. I hope and pray we all make it."

We sat for a while, not saying anything more until Kate woke up from her nap.

"I'll get her," Rick got up to check her.

I sat there by myself. The thought of demons running through the streets was a frightening concept. But we had to be strong and keep remembering there was only one way to handle them. We had to be earnest in prayer.

∽

Joanne spent the day in the same fashion. She was busy asking John to start boarding up the slider doors in their family room. Jess was busy working on her scrapbook and pasting pictures in it.

"That ought to do it!" John nailed the last of the nails into the wood.

"Let's see if there's anything happening on TV," Joanne wanted to sit down.

It was early evening now and the sun had set. Nothing of great importance was happening in the news. Jess got ready for bed and went upstairs to her room to watch a movie. John locked up the downstairs and joined his wife to watch TV in their bedroom. All was quiet and peaceful, like the calm before the storm.

"Why don't you stay home from work tomorrow John, just until we have some definite news about this situation?" Joanne asked him.

"I can't take anymore time off or they'll fire me. I've already used up all of my vacation time," he saw her concern. "Don't worry sweetheart, I'll be all right. I'm not that far away. If anything starts to happen I can be home in about ten minutes."

"I'd feel better if you were here. You know what Jill told us about people traveling when the three days begin."

"There's going to be another warning before the days begin, remember?" he tried to reassure her.

John reached to hold her and cuddle her in his arms until she gave in and agreed with him.

"I think I'll grab a shower now so I can sleep in a little later in the morning," he smiled at her.

They kissed each other and John headed off for the bathroom. Joanne pulled out her Bible. She was accustomed to read it every night before she went to bed. It was no different this night. John went into the bathroom and closed the door. He went over to the window and was about to pull the shade down when he glanced out into the backyard and up at the evening sky. He looked at the moon.

"What the . . . ?" he blurted out. Then he managed to shout out to Joanne, "Hey Jo, can you come here for a minute?"

Joanne made her way over to the bathroom door and knocked on it. John opened the door right away.

"Come here for a moment," he led her over to the window. "Look at the moon. What do you see?"

Joanne looked out over the black trees to the moon. It was full and was shining brightly.

"That's odd," she noticed that the moon's rays weren't shining out in a full circle around it. Rather the rays were shining out from east to west and from north to south. "It looks like a Cross," she told him.

"Yeah, that's what I see. Is this the Cross in the sky we're supposed to look for?"

They looked shocked at each other for a moment. "I'm not sure," Joanne answered him. "I'm going to call Jill."

She left John at the window and went back into the bedroom to use the phone.

"Jill? I'm sorry to bother you, but I want you to go look out your window at the moon. I'll wait."

I went to look out the back windows of our house. It was an eerie sight to see rays of the moon pointing north to south and east to west. I called for Rick to look too. He was as startled as I was. I got back on the phone.

"Yes, Joanne, I looked. It looks like a Cross."

"Do you think this is the last sign?" she asked me.

"I'm not sure. It's not bitterly cold, but I'll keep an eye out."

"Me too. I just wanted to warn you. I'm going to bed now. I'll talk to you tomorrow."

We hung up the telephones. It was late and Rick and I were tired. We got into bed. The two of us stayed awake for a little while trying to make sense of the phenomenon going on over our backyard.

"Why would the moon shine like that, in the form of a Cross?" I wondered.

"Keep an eye out now," was all Rick could say.

We held each other close to ease each other's fears. Then we fell fast asleep.

I awoke during the night grabbing for the extra quilt on the bed. I was freezing. I wondered if Rick had left the air conditioner on full blast. He liked keeping things cool. I got out of bed to check it, but it was turned off. Rick stirred a little. Next, I went to the bathroom. I looked outside again to check the moon. I noticed half the moon was now gone! There was a black ink seeming to cover it! Just then the alarm clock went off. It was morning but things were looking rather dark. I couldn't fathom what was happening for a few moments. I was entranced by the moon disappearing in the black sky. I was shivering. Rick awoke looking at the clock. He was a little startled to find the room so dark that morning. He took another look at the clock and this time he noticed both the hands of the clock were moving quickly round and round to all the numbers as if time were speeding up and going haywire.

"What's going on?" he shivered.

"Turn on the TV!" I hurried back into the room.

I immediately saw a breaking story taking place in Europe. It was midday there and crowds of people were gathered in darkened streets looking up to the sky. They were trying to figure out why an eclipse was taking place when there wasn't supposed to be one occurring. They were mesmerized pointing and looking up. The camera pointed to the darkening sky as well. Slowly like the blackest of inks the horizons were being engulfed and the sky was blackening all around them. It was almost like night and people were screaming and running.

"It's the end of the world!" a man shouted.

At which point the camera disconnected and there was no further picture. I turned to another channel. Each channel was fading from view.

"Grab the kids!" I screamed.

"What's happening?" Rick sat upright in bed.

"Just do as I say! Hurry!" I was frantic. I ran to the phone to try to warn Joanne. There was tons of static over the lines. When she answered the phone she could barely hear me.

"Seek shelter! This is it! God be with you!" I tried to tell her.

"Jill is that you?" Joanne screamed back into the phone. But it was no use. I couldn't make out what she was saying.

The phone lines were breaking up. "John's left for work! Can you hear me? He isn't here! Jill? Jill?"

Then the phone just went dead.

Rick was standing in the darkening hallway of our upstairs with all the kids. The children were rubbing their eyes. They were still half asleep.

"To the basement at once!" I commanded them to listen.

Just then Rick understood what was happening. "Come on Ricky run!" he shouted.

I checked all the doors and windows to make sure everything was locked. I pulled a few shades down too. There was not a moment to spare. Darkness was enveloping the whole house. We could barely see in front of ourselves!

"Hurry!" I kept yelling. "Hurry!"

The kids ran quickly as Rick carried baby Kate in his arms. I was last getting everyone into our little laundry room then pulling the door shut and locking it. It was getting darker and darker more quickly by the moment.

"Where are the candles?" I shouted to Rick. I was shaking with fear that we'd be left in the pitch dark.

Rick began feeling around on the shelves. "I got one!" he shouted out loud.

"Light it, hurry! Light it!" I screamed.

Rick's hands were shaking as he struck the match to the matchbox trying to get the match to light. Suddenly it ignited and he found the wick to the blessed candle. He lit it. There was a tiny bit of light in the tiny room.

☙❧

Meanwhile the Sullivan and the Nelson households were frantically lighting their blessed candles too. Everyone from church was aware of what was happening and was trying to seek shelter in their room of refuge. The *Three Days of Darkness* were about to commence.

Mr. Sullivan was trying frantically to light his candle. "Come on! Come on!" he kept trying over and over.

"Hurry!" Maureen called out to him. "It's almost totally dark!"

"I'm trying. It won't light!"

"Is there someone here who doesn't believe what is happening?" Maureen shouted.

One of the boys had been skeptical but upon hearing his mother's tone of voice readily believed in what was happening.

"There we go!" the candle lit. It was just in the nick of time.

❦

The Enrich house was becoming darker and darker with every second. At long last Dave began looking for the candle Margaret Nelson had offered him. He stumbled in the darkness looking frantically for it.

"I know it's here someplace," he felt the walls, the shelves, the countertops. Moving about wildly in the darkness he finally came upon the prized possession and tried to light it. Over and over he struck the matches. Over and over the matches went out.

"Come on! Come on!" he tried in vain. His hopes were fading as he came to the last match. "This is it!" he tried for the last time. He struck the match and tried to hold it to the blessed candle's wick. "Come on! Light! Light!" he cursed. But the match burned down to the end and would not light. He sat there alone in almost total blackness.

❦

Susan and Ed had gone away for a few days visiting relatives. They had gotten an early start back home the day the sky was beginning to darken.

"Look Ed, all the lights are going out!" Susan noticed.
Lights began to go out everywhere around them. Traffic
began to get tied up. Street lights were going out as if there
was a power outage.

"Great! I thought we'd get home early today. Looks like
we're gonna sit in traffic," Ed complained.

People were conversing, "What do you make of it?"

"What can this mean?"

Traffic jams began to occur. They couldn't get by them.

Suddenly Susan began to recall her neighbor's warnings.
"Ed, do think this could be the start of the three days of . . ."
Susan's voice was shaky.

But it was too late now. There was no place to run to, no
place to hide.

Everyone got out of their car and looked up just as the
last rays of light disappeared from view. Suddenly they were
engulfed in total darkness!

Screams were heard all around them as everyone began
to fall to the ground. In a matter of moments everything was
silent.

Then Ed and Sue fell as well. All of them died instantly!

Chapter 7

John had left for work while it was still dark out. He had to get to work early. But noticing something definitely wrong with the sky he turned about face and drove directly home. He had been warned of the grim consequences for all those who were traveling when the *Three Days of Darkness* would begin.

Joanne was out of her mind with worry. She grabbed Jess and hugged her in their family room. They had already lit their blessed candles.

"Joanne! Joanne! Quick let me in!" John pounded on the door.

"John? Is that you?" Joanne almost grabbed to open the door, then she hesitated. She turned to Jess, "Jill told us not to talk to anyone outside."

"It's me! Please, for the love of God, open the door!" he shouted.

Jess looked scared. She wanted to let her dad in, but she wasn't really sure it was him.

"Sprinkle holy water around the door," Jess whispered to Joanne.

They sprinkled the water and still heard John pounding, "Let me in! Please Jo, it's really me!"

Joanne rushed at the door and turning her eyes, so as not to look out, told Jess to close her eyes as well. Then she flung open the door and John rushed inside.

"Quick, shut the door!" he was shaking.

Joanne and Jess quickly embraced him.

"Oh, thank God! Thank God, you're safe!" They all hugged each other.

"How did you survive being out there?" Joanne looked at her husband.

John began to weep, "I saw the morning sky suddenly become more and more black. It was so weird. The sky had been such a nice light shade of blue but was slowly being stained by what looked like the blackest of inks creeping up from every vantage point along the horizon. I immediately turned the car right around and came home. It was getting so black, darker and darker by the moment. By the time I made it to our garage everything was near total blackness. So I shut my eyes and felt my way in. I didn't open my eyes!"

"Oh, thank God. I thought you were . . ." Joanne just kept hugging him. "Never mind, you're safe now!"

We were all shaking and trying to get our wits about us. Nothing of this sort had ever happened before. There was no light, except for our blessed candles, and that light was even a little eerie because it was so very black. The children were frightened huddling close to us for support and to keep warm. It grew terribly cold. I quickly wrapped each of them in an oversized comforter and rocked them gently. Kate was still asleep in her little car seat. I was relieved we were all together. I quickly said a prayer for John and Joanne. I hoped that all was right at their house as well.

And then the hauntings began, very subtle at first, then growing rather loud. I was rocking Rachel in my arms and trying to sing her a little lullaby when Rick silenced me trying to hear something. We all became very quiet.

There was a faint noise, like a little humming sound, like the sound of a bee's swarm from a distance.

"Listen!" Rick tried to hear what it was.

We waited and listened as the sound grew steadily louder and louder coming closer and closer. Suddenly it became as if a great train or a tornado was just outside our door! The noise was tremendous nearly deafening to our ears. We had to cover our ears fearing they would pop with the horrid sounds. A great pounding came to the laundry room door as if a great number of strong men were trying to smash it in!

"Open the door!" the evil intruders ordered us. "You don't stand a chance of surviving!" Then a most wicked and evil laugh came forth, one I had never heard before.

The children screamed of fright and I too was afraid of what was happening.

I tried to scream to Rick, "Sprinkle the holy water!"

But even though he was only a couple of feet away he couldn't hear me. I got up from my spot and reached for the jug of holy water off the shelf. The noise almost made me double over. The laughter from outside was hideous. It was relentless. I quickly opened the jug of the most precious water and flung some at the door. There was an immediate response. A vapor like steam floated in around the cracks of the door. The laughter turned to howls of anguish and the pounding seemed to subside. I continued to splash the water all over the entire door. The enemy was slowly retreating. I could hear them scampering away.

"Who is like unto God?" I shouted through the door.

They seemed to go a short distance from the locked door then convened for a moment to plot out their next course of action. One of them stayed behind to try the doorknob, shaking it gently at first, then rattling it fiercely in great efforts to get the door open!

I looked up at the shelf and noticed the statue of the Blessed Mother. I quickly remembered that Father had told us to have recourse to her.

"Let's say the rosary!" I yelled to everyone.

Rick and I passed around a container of the beads as each of the children took one and blessed themselves, "In the name of the Father, and of the Son, and of the Holy Ghost, Amen . . ." We began in earnest to pray.

There was a great cry and bitter lamentation from outside the door at the onset of beginning those prayers. The more we prayed the greater the anguish until it began to fade away from where we were. There seemed to be a little silence again. But it was a false sense of security.

Meanwhile, the Sullivans were having their own set of problems. They were reading from their Bible when they were interrupted by a stenchful kind of smell. It smelled like rotting corpses and horrid gases like ammonia and sulphur. It came upon them suddenly and filled the house with the most putrid aroma. Colleen began to choke. Mary Alice followed her and so on down the line until everyone was choking or ready to vomit.

Mrs. Sullivan thought it may be poisonous remembering that Father McGrath told them the demons would release poisonous vapors and gases into the air. But protection would come to the elect. Mrs. Sullivan told her children to prostrate themselves like crosses on the floor and pray that way with outstretched arms. Gagging and struggling to breathe, the children one by one laid down on the floor. Falling so low, they found that the smell wasn't as putrid on the ground. Rather the air was cleaner and easier to breathe. The gas seemed to be rising and floating up to the ceiling. They began to pray more earnestly and in thanksgiving that the Lord was protecting them and sheltering them from the abuse of their enemies.

"Let us give thanks to Almighty God for the protection He has provided us with," Mr. Sullivan shouted out for his family to hear as well as the demons on the outside of their house.

But Jimmy wasn't paying attention to what his father was saying. He was curious about the demons outside. He seemed lured by their tricks. Growing braver from the initial shock of the onset of the *Three Days of Darkness*, he began to wander off, wanting to look out a window. Mrs. Sullivan spotted him trying to pull back the shade in the adjacent room.

"Jimmy!" she shouted after him.

Mr. Sullivan looked up seeing Jimmy standing alone and near the window.

"Come here, son!" he tried to coax him back to where they all were. But the boy seemed like he was in a trance. He didn't seem to snap out of it. It was as if he were in another world far from where his family was. He wasn't listening to them, didn't care what they were doing and seemed defiant as to their suggestions to come back and join them.

"Jimmy please, in the name of God!" Mrs. Sullivan held her rosary beads tightly. She stretched out her arms in his direction hoping for him to run to her. "Mary, great Mother of God, help us!" she uttered out loud.

At the name of Mary the trance seemed to lift off of the child and he came to his senses. Hearing everyone calling for him, he ran back to the room his family was in and joining them he laid down on the floor prostrating in prayer. Mrs. Sullivan began to cry. Mary Alice cried too seeing her mother so distraught. Mr. Sullivan tried to comfort them holding them and telling them everything was going to be all right to which the demons mocked him.

"You're a liar! Things will not be all right! Things will get much worse! You're just beginning to be punished! Do you think this is over yet? Not by a long run!" and then a most wicked and cunning laugh rang out over and over. The sound of that laughter echoed throughout the house, shaking the foundation to the very core. The scared family huddled together for strength and support.

The Nelson household was much the same. Mr. Nelson was pretty much confined to his chair, while Mrs. Nelson sat very close to him shivering with fear. They hadn't yet made it to their den. They were silent, listening to the sounds going on all around them. There was a little clawing, gnawing, scratching sound near the outside doorway. It seemed to begin at the bottom of the door and slowly move its way up. The scratching continued with the sound of sharp nails and sharp teeth moving across the door then up and down. It seemed to be studying the door, looking for a way to open it. A second set of scratching commenced. There were whispers going on, as if the demons were devising a plan, then more scratching. It seemed the more they searched across the door for an opening the more frustrated they became. Margaret grabbed on to Don as the unwelcome visitors tried to turn the door knob unsuccessfully. Then the sound of cursing and frustrations mounted.

"They have locked their door!"

"What shall we do now?"

"We'll try the windows!"

"Let us destroy everything! Let us devour them! Let us drag their worthless bodies through the streets!" an evil voice kept demanding.

The evil conversations continued, as Margaret and Don huddled quietly together. The clawing sounds seemed to scale the walls of their house even reaching the upstairs windows without having stairs to get to them! They began again trying to open the locked windows. The scratching was constant and deliberate. The demons were determined to gain entrance. The noise was relentless driving Don and Margaret to the brink of insanity, when suddenly Margaret could stand no more and she shouted out, "Stop it! Stop it, I say!"

To which an evil laugh rang out more wicked than anything they had ever heard before! It was more frightening than the scratching. Margaret hid her face in Don's shoulder not wanting to look at what might happen next.

"She told us to stop! As if we care! We shall *never* stop! Hear us! We won't stop until you're all dead! Keep on trying to get them!" the scratching was more powerful and it seemed more demons came to join the others in their wicked efforts.

Suddenly a glass broke upstairs and Margaret could hear the sound of little footsteps coming in and running madly about the upstairs floor. More and more footsteps seemed to follow until it began to sound like a stampede! The uninvited visitors were frantic to find where Margaret and Don were.

Margaret got up quickly and very quietly helped her husband towards the den. Slowly they stepped. Quietly they made their way. Margaret could hardly breathe she was so frightened. She edged her way. She tried very hard not to make even the slightest sound. Don tried very hard not to make a sound either. He felt so helpless to do anything for his wife. Then a great stillness filled the house. Don realized that the demons were on to them and were zeroing in for where to attack.

"Quick Margaret! Shut the door now!" Don screamed.

Margaret leaped for the door anxious to close it, but there were claws everywhere about the open door!

"Quick Don! The holy water! Get me some holy water!" Margaret cried out trying to push the door closed.

The water was right beside Don's chair in the den on the floor. He grabbed for it in an instant! Then even though his fingers fumbled with the lid, he quickly opened the bottle and with all his might flung a huge amount towards the door. Immediately there was release from the opposite side of the door. The claws quickly withdrew. The devils ceased trying to force their way in. A steam or vapor quickly ensued from the cracks around the doorway. There was cursing and howling so dreadful that Margaret had to cover her ears lest she faint. She managed to get back to where Don was still sitting and took the bottle of holy water from him and began to sprinkle the windows in that room as well. All the while Don kept reciting the Pater Noster.

It must have been the same in every house. Demons all over the world were trying to break in and murder people by tearing them to bits in fits of great rage. The streets that were once filled with people and cars were all completely in chaos. There were no human sounds of any kind heard outside. Birds and crickets could not be heard. There was nothing to remind us of an ordinary day.

But we hardly had the time to think about how everyone else was faring. We certainly had troubles of our own and right after the first close encounter with the wicked demons from hell, came a second attack, more alarming than the first.

The children were crying. They were frightened. We were all frightened. But I tried to remember what Father had told us about discouragement. He said the demons would strike when we were tired or discouraged. And so it seemed when things were in chaos or at their worst a new attack would get underway. I had to calm the kids and get our wits about us in order to do battle and keep us safe and focused. I looked up at the Blessed Mother statue. It seemed to bow in agreement to me. Was it really bowing or had I just imagined it?

"Look at the statue!" I called out to everyone.

"It's moving!" Ricky said.

"It is moving!" Rick confirmed it.

"How can a statue move?" Rachel became more and more alarmed.

"I'm not sure, honey," I couldn't take my eyes off the statue.

Then the statue began to rise right off of the shelf and towards the ceiling.

"Pray!" I shouted out loud. "Pray with all your might!"

We began in earnest to recite the rosary. At the start of these prayers the statue quickly fell from its height and I grabbed it just before it almost hit the floor. Seems the devil wanted to divert our attention in some way by using the statue to get our attention. But what were they up to now?

We could hear them rushing about all along the outsides of our house. They were angry, enraged, and they wanted us to perish.

I heard a strong gruffy voice shout out, "Try all the windows and doors! There must be a way! If you can't get in that way, use the chimney! But get them, every last one of them!"

Immediately there was a sound like that of a volcanic eruption! With this explosion of hatred and determination came tremendous banging sounds! Bricks were dismantled from our chimney and fell all over the place, giving way to legions of demons who sought entrance to our house from the upstairs!

"I didn't sprinkle the windows upstairs with holy water," I whispered to Rick.

The next thing we heard was the sound of breaking glass. It sounded like every window in the house had been broken. There was a rush of wind so violent and penetrating we shook just hearing that sound. Next came a sound like an army of invaders trampling through our living room. I could hear things smashing and breaking. These invaders were vicious screaming out in rage as they seemed to be searching for something of greater importance, namely *us*!

"Pray!" I whispered so that the demons wouldn't hear me.

We all began praying, but in spite of our prayers, we heard footsteps marching and running overhead. They wanted us and they wanted us quite badly. Everything was so completely dark except for the candles that still gave off a very eerie bluish light. The children were petrified. I tried to comfort them.

"Remember," I whispered, "when we had those last few thunderstorms?"

The children quickly nodded that they did.

"Well, do you remember when the lights went out?"

Rick was catching on to where I was going with this.

"Well, let's just pretend it's a very bad storm outside," Rick interjected.

"Yes, it's so bad that it knocked down our big oak tree out front and smashed all our windows!" I said.

Rick added, "And we'll have to get them fixed when the storm passes."

"And just think . . ."

The demons heard us talking softly and in a fit of rage raced to our laundry room door pushing and shoving one another. Each one was hoping to be the first to come upon us.

"Just think . . ." I tried to continue.

The demons were at the door again trying the knob with great agitation. It was locked tight and they couldn't hold it for long. It had been blessed with holy water.

"Just think, that Daniel left the TV on full blast and there's an adventure movie on, or a scary movie playing, and that it's all make-believe. It's not really happening. It's all make-believe . . ."

To which came a dreadful reply, "Make-believe! Ha ha ha ha!" The demons were sarcastic and angry. "We're not finished with you yet! Not by a long run! You won't stay safe in that room for three days. You won't stay safe in that room for one more hour! Our intelligence is far more crafty than yours. And we're far more resourceful than you! We'll kill every one of you and drag you back to hell with us!"

We shuttered at those words. Daniel was getting braver believing it was all pretend.

"You don't scare me!" he shouted back at them.

It enraged them all at once. I'm not sure why. I wondered if it was because Daniel was so defiant of their threats or perhaps because he was still so innocent and childlike that they hated him with such a vengeance. In any case they pounded on the door with such an impact that it seemed to almost split the door into pieces!

"Don't talk to them!" I yelled over the noise. "Remember what Father McGrath told us. He said not to talk to anyone outside. Let's read from the Bible. Here's a story about a great warrior. His name was David. And even though he was just a boy, small and humble in stature, he slew Goliath who was a giant . . ."

This really enraged the beasts. But they realized they were foiled by the blessed door and their being ignored and by our reading Sacred Scripture. They decided to go off a safe distance from us and convene with some sinister plans as to how they were going to overpower us.

In the meanwhile, Mr. Enrich was left in the pitch darkness. His candle never lit. He was a scoffer who didn't believe in such things as the *Three Days of Darkness*. He went along with the idea only to please Mrs. Nelson. He didn't think he would actually use the blessed candle she gave him. He was regrettably shaken now that he had doubted her. He wasn't a bad man. He had some admirable qualities about him. He was first to lend a helping hand for those in need. He sang in the church choir. He went to church every Sunday and even on Holy Days. He helped his neighbors. But the one thing he should have taken seriously he did not. Now he was forced to endure the predicament he was in.

As he sat in the center of his living room he could hear the scratching and the gnawing at his doors. They were locked. He could hear the tiny sounds of a million footsteps climbing up the walls and the roof. It sounded like a parade of spiders or crabs. He sat very still careful not to make a sound of his own. He was terrified.

There was a window left wide open upstairs and the demons had found it that way even in the darkness. They laughed a loud sinister laugh, one so cruel it sent shivers down poor Mr. Enrich's spine.

"This is going to be a piece of cake!" he heard one of the more terrible of the demons speak.

"Dave?" a softer evil voice rang out. "We know you're in here. Come out so we can find you. You can't hide from us. Not for very long, that is."

Mr. Enrich was dripping with sweat even though it was extremely cold. His heart was racing, pounding with fear. There was no one he could turn to for help. There was no one around. He didn't know whether he should just stay put where he was or make a mad dash for it to one of the downstairs rooms. He sat for what seemed like ages trying to decide, when suddenly he heard the destruction of his furniture and belongings being thrashed and broken into bits by a wild and unruly army of mighty warriors.

Room after room they were relentless. He could hear them lifting the beds and throwing them through the walls. The crashing sounds and the splintering of woods rang out in the turmoil. Glass was breaking and objects were being thrown everywhere. He could hear papers being torn over and over again. They were probably his treasured photos or important documents he had in safe keeping. Wicked laughter resounded throughout his home.

These wicked invaders were delighted causing such chaos but were harboring greater hopes of ending it all with murder! There was no relief in sight. The laughter, the destruction, the evil sounds all drove Dave to make a mad dash for the downstairs parlor. He slammed the door quickly locking it behind him. The house suddenly went totally silent.

Dave stayed by the door, holding it with his body, listening against it to see where his enemies were or what they were up to. The sweat was dripping off of him. He tried to think about how he was going to get through three days of this and stay alive.

"We know where you are, Dave!" came a creepy voice in the darkness.

Dave cringed in fear, "You'll never take me alive!" he yelled back in defiance at them.

"That's what you think!" an uglier voice echoed back.

An ill wind started to blow and a smell so stenchful and horrid started to fill the room Dave was in. Dave stepped away from the door. He had no defense. He had no holy water. There was no light. He didn't have a rosary in his pocket. There were no statues for him to gaze at. He was all alone and helpless. He ran for the telephone to try and call someone, anyone, just to hear the voice of a friend. But the phone wasn't working. He ran to switch on a light. But the lights weren't working. Nothing was working.

His life began to flash before his eyes. He saw his sins. He was afraid to look at how he had offended God, but it was no use. The sands of the hourglass were slowly being emptied for him.

"Remember when you stole that piece of candy at the dime store when you were ten?" came a terrifying voice.

"Remember when you cheated your boss at work about your hours?" came a grueling whisper.

"Remember when your neighbors tried to warn you about these days?" another horrifying demon laughed.

All of his faults and sins were being told to him over and over. They were soft then became louder and louder until it was almost deafening. One by one the insults and the animosities were shouted out to him. And with each reminder, Dave cringed and fell to the floor. He curled himself up into a little ball and began to weep. His life flashed before him and a terrible griping pain seized his chest. He felt as though he was having a heart attack. But the pain was nothing compared to his fear.

The demons were at the door, all of them, and then in one swift motion they burst into the room where poor Dave laid in waiting and in the course of an instant devoured him!

Chapter 8

It seemed like we had been in that locked room in the basement for ages. The sounds and tortures of the demons had already taken so much out of us. I looked down at my wrist watch to see if I could tell what time it was and all I could make out was the hour and minute hands swirling madly about the face of the watch in opposite directions! There was no rhyme or reason to this unexplainable enigma. The only thing I could think of was that the world was in complete chaos since hell had been completely emptied.

My thoughts turned to Joanne and John for a moment. I was hoping they were safe. I wondered if they would come through this ordeal, or if we all would. I wondered how many people were perishing in the darkness. And I wondered what the earth would be like once it had been cleansed of its sins. I looked over at the burning candles. The wax in the glass jars had melted down only about a quarter of an inch or so. That was only a few hours of time. I began to realize the melted wax was the only way to tell how much time had passed. We still had a long way to go.

Just then a soft eerie kind of song began to break through the sudden stillness.

"Ah, ahhh, ah, ahhh" its pitch was in a very ugly C minor and quite frightening. It seemed to linger right outside our door. It sounded like a female sighing but we could tell she was not just some ordinary lady. She sounded seductive and wicked. We waited wondering what would happen next.

Her song grew louder and became rather violent and angry. It was meant to frighten us. All the hauntings were meant to frighten us. That was the primary goal of the demons, to frighten to death or simply to cause death to every man, woman and child left on earth! They were hungry for souls not having had this much dominion over the earth in quite sometime. And they were wicked in their attempts. There was no reasoning with them. They were on a mission to seek revenge on all of mankind. They were savagely angry at God for being thrown out of Heaven and then seeing men fill up their emptied thrones instead. The war raged onward.

I began to sing a hymn from church, "Ave, Ave, Ave Maria. Ave, Ave, Maria! . . ." and the children knowing the hymn joined in with me to drown out the sickening sounds behind our door.

As we got louder to overpower the gruesome sounds, so did that demon in her response to us. We continued to sing outright and proudly. There was no stopping us. A great slam pounded our door!

"Shut up! Shut Up! I hate you! I hate you all! But I hate you the most Jill, because you started this!" the witch screamed into our room. "I'll be after *you!*"

I kept singing.

"Aren't you going to say anything to her?" Daniel asked me.

"There's nothing to answer, my precious little treasure," and I smiled at him as best I could wanting to keep him calm and trying to remain unafraid.

A great shriek and a very loud scream ensued next. "Who do you think *you* are?" she became enraged. "How dare you ignore me? Don't you know who I am? Open this door at once you worthless little bitch! I'm going to tear you to pieces!"

I grabbed the holy water and sprinkled the door again. There was a loud singeing sound that occurred at the same moment. A vapor rose from under the door and a piercing scream was released into the dark blackened air. A strong gust of wind followed that nearly extinguished the candles. Rick jumped up at once to try to save our light. He was frantic not to let the candles go out, lest we be in total darkness.

"Who is like unto God?" he shouted out.

"Shut up! Shut your putrid mouths! You make me sick! You pompous little scum! You're worthless, I tell you! You'll never see the light of day!"

"Those candles won't go out. Don't you remember what Father told us? He said once lit the candles won't go out in the houses of the elect. We are the elect, Rick. Take courage and have no fear."

I got strength from remembering Father's own words and I felt a renewed confidence as I opened the Bible again. This time I started reading at the beginning, and was prepared to read from Genesis to the Apocalypse before I put the book down.

"In the beginning God created Heaven, and earth. And the earth was void and empty, and darkness was upon the face of the deep: and the spirit of God moved over the waters. And God said, be light made. And light was made." . . .

Joanne helped John to hold the door to their family room shut while Jess flung holy water at the savage spirits that were trying to force their way in. Finally the enemy subsided and they managed to shut and lock the door. But the evil ones didn't go away happily. They were enraged that they had been shut out and had come away without a lost soul. A great deal of conversations were going on, devising a plan to overpower Joanne's family as soon as they let their guard down.

In the meantime, Jess had opened a spiritual book about St. Joan. It was a beautiful blue leather book describing and telling all about Joan's features, her looks and her life. She began to read out loud some of the words regarding the Hundred Years War between France and Great Britain.

"Jeanne was born in the 15th century . . ." Jess continued. "She was born January 6, 1412, to be exact, the feast of the Epiphany. She lived in the tiny village of Domremy in France. She was also baptized there by Jean Minet with numerous godfathers and godmothers present . . ."

Jess tried to keep reading but she was constantly being interrupted by noises of every kind and the foulest of smells one could ever imagine. The smell was enough to gag even the toughest of men. It was overpowering. No one could be certain if it came from one of the beasts or many of them. It seemed to linger and almost become absorbed into the taste buds. Jess dropped her book and coughed trying to gasp for air.

"You were doing fine!" Joanne tried to coax her to relax. She picked up the book and tried to resume where Jess had left off.

"Let me see here," Joanne turned a few pages. "Oh yes, here we are. It says Saint Joan . . ."

"Enough about *her*!" came a very gruff reply from outside their door. "We hate *her* so much! We tried to upset her victories in France, legend that *she* was! *We hate her! We hate her!* Do you hear us? Stop reading about *her* at once!" A terrible scraping sound began at the door and a pounding and pushing that seemed to almost break the door off its hinges.

"Dad!" Jess ran to grab hold of her father.

"It's all right Jess, there's nothing to fear. We've come this far already."

"Ha ha ha ha ha!" a great deal of sarcastic laughter ensued from behind the locked door. "They think they have come a great way! You will die in the next few minutes!" the chieftain of liars shouted back to them.

Jess couldn't hold back any longer. She let out a blood curdling scream which seemed to entice the evil invaders to disrupt things all the more, causing havoc and chaos at her terror. They stamped their claw-like feet! They banged, broke, and threw things! There was a great rumbling sound.

Joanne tried to look up from her huddled position.

"Who is like unto God?" she blurted out in the meekest of manner, for her terror had drained her of her fortitude.

Little did she know that her meekness caused their enemies to take flight because demons dread those who are humbled before God. And demons especially fear the great Mother of God who is the most humble of all creatures. They became worried that Mary may come to their assistance. So they hurried off to plan a new course of attack.

One had to be very careful not to fall into the snares these demons made, for they were crude, cunning and quite intelligent beings. It was so important to remember everything Father McGrath had told them. Following his instruction was the key to surviving this terrible ordeal.

"Saint Dominic was on his way to Rome to see the Pope when he was held up by robbers in Fanjeaux. Immediately seeing that these robbers were about to kill him for his riches, he fell to his knees and begged them to torture him to his death! He wanted to die imitating Our Lord on the Cross. The robbers gasped at such madness and quickly fled leaving him alone." . . . Patrick Sullivan read to his family.

"I'm tired," James whined.

"And I'm hungry!" Mary Alice complained.

They had been fighting the good fight for so long now that the urges of the human body needed refreshing.

"I'll fix you something," Mrs. Sullivan got up to check her supply of canned goods. "I have . . ."

This stirred trouble outside the door.

"They're hungry!"

"They're tired!"

"Let's tear them to pieces!"

"Wait!" one very cunning demon surmised. "They're tired, did you hear that? When they tire they make mistakes. Our opportunity may be coming sooner than we think. Let's not be too hasty in our efforts to take them all now. Let us wait a little longer, even though this is hard for us to do. Our waiting may be more profitable in the long run."

"I have to go to the bathroom," Patrick got up matter-of-factly and headed straight for the door to go to the bathroom. He had his hand on the doorknob and turned it to open the door. A blast of putrid air filled their room as Mr. Sullivan jumped to his feet and ordered James to stop!

Before James could look out or go out of their blessed room Mr. Sullivan quickly closed and locked the door again.

"Jimmy, my boy, you can't leave this room," he tried to explain to him. "It's just not safe anymore. We have to stay here together until these three days are over. No one is to open this door," he turned around to face the rest of his family. "No one under any circumstances is to leave this room! Do you all hear me?"

He needed to shout as there was a great deal of commotion outside again. The devils had missed there chance to bombard the room when Jimmy opened the door.

Margaret Nelson was trying to open a can of baked beans for her husband and herself but was having trouble with the manual can opener.

"We didn't realize how convenient things were for us, did we?" she tried to smile as she struggled.

"Here, let me have a try at it," Don said. He was hungry now as well.

As he grasped the tool opening the can for her he noticed a rather strange sound coming from upstairs in their house. It was subtle at first, but then it became more audible. Margaret was about to say something to her husband when he silenced her and ordered her to listen.

"Oh Don," a young woman's voice said teasingly, "We shouldn't."

A young man's voice whispered loudly, "Come on Jen, you know you want to."

At which point Mr. Nelson sat up straight. He was listening to his distant past, as if it had been recorded and was now being played back. Margaret could hear everything too! He tried to shout over it not wanting his wife to hear. But it was too late. The sounds of this seduction seemed to ring out throughout the house. Moans and groans of pleasure and vulgarities were heard.

"Stop it! Stop it!" he shouted for the torments to stop.

Then there was a creaking sound and the sound of footsteps coming down the stairs. They walked right over to the den door and knocked gently.

"Who's there?" Margaret asked.

"It's me, Jen. I know you're in there Don. Come on now, open up for me. You know you want to. I'm so cold out here. Just let me come in for a little while."

Mr. Nelson remembered back to a peaceful time in his life when he was just a young boy. Jen was his first love and his feelings ran very deep for her. He was rekindling his imagination with thoughts of her as he debated whether or not to open the door.

"Who is Jen?" Margaret turned to her husband.

"She's an old girlfriend of mine. We . . . I . . . ." he couldn't finish his thought. He couldn't tell her they had plans to marry.

He didn't want to awaken those feelings he had tried so hard to suppress for all those years.

"I'm so cold, Don. Please open the door. I need your arms around me," she tried to seduce him.

"Keep focused on what we were doing!" he shouted to his wife. "Here! Here is our dinner! Eat the beans!"

"You never told me about a Jen," Margaret began her discourse. "Who was she?" she asked him again. There was a feeling of jealousy building and an argument was about to erupt between them. This was precisely what the evil ones had desired.

Don was already eating his food, without having said Grace before his meal, without praying at all for any assistance. He was falling right into the careful trap that was being laid out for him. His hunger had fled and he was desirous of his lost love, but he kept forcing the beans into his mouth.

"Come on Don, just hold me. You know you want to. I'm dying to see you again. Let me come in, please sweetheart. Please open the door for me."

Margaret was becoming all the more furious at the intruder's remarks and her wicked suggestions.

"If you won't let her in, I will!" Margaret got to her feet and stormed for the door.

"Don't let her in! Don't open that door!" Don shouted to his wife, helpless to get up and stop her.

"I have a thing or two to say to this hussy!" Margaret shouted back to him.

"Disagreements! How lucky we are!" Margaret could hear whispering coming directly outside. "Go on Jen, have her open the door for us!"

Margaret's hand was on the doorknob when she suddenly pulled back.

"Don't open the door," Don pleaded. "In the name of God, don't open it!"

Margaret stopped. She looked down to the floor. She was crushed thinking that she had been the one and only love of

Don's for all their years. She had been lied to. She just stood there.

Don looked over to where his wife stood, "I'm sorry Margaret. I'm so sorry. I love you more than anything else in this world. Please forgive me. Please, honey."

"Oh come on Don, don't be so foolish," Jen's voice echoed back into the room. "We can pick up where we left off. There's no stopping us now!"

"Stop it! Stop it, I say! Stay away from us! Go away! You're not welcome here! Do you hear me! Go away!" Margaret pounded on the door. Then she slowly crumbled to the floor crushed with sorrow. Don tried with all his might to get out of his chair and go to the assistance of his wife.

He managed to reach her using all his efforts and got down on the ground beside her and cuddled her in his arms.

"What are you doing? Don? What are you doing?" Jen's voice became frantic.

A great love filled the room where Don and Margaret were. There was no denying that their love was true and real. The demons couldn't stand it! Even though the Nelson's had forgotten their prayers for a little while, their love was a prayer most pleasing and acceptable to God.

"Love conquers a multitude of sins," Margaret whispered.

"And I do love you," Don replied.

"No! No! No!" came a pounding on their door with curses and shrieking in a frenzy. A trembling sound followed with a stampede of demons fleeing that place for fear of having to witness real love and feel the emanating effects of it.

There was no way to adjust or get used to the relentless tauntings of the demons. There was no time to feel secure, which made Rick and me overly cautious in this regard. We continued to read, continued to pray and sang hymns. In between we added ejaculations to praise God. But I could see the children were hungry and baby Kate began to cry as well.

We had to settle for juice boxes for our choice of drinks. There was no way to chill anything in a refrigerator. No appliances were working. I poured a container into a bottle for baby Kate and she immediately was happy when she put it in her mouth. Then I began making little peanut butter sandwiches with the Ritz crackers I had left on the shelf.

As I worked, Rick was reciting the rosary out loud so we could all hear it and respond accordingly to the prayers. There wasn't a moment to spare in saying prayers. They had to be said, needed to be said, to keep the enemy at bay.

Just then the room seemed to get a little darker in a sense even though the candles were still burning their eerie glow. We all noticed it and took heed to it. We weren't sure what was going to happen next. It was subtle at first, the tiny scratching fluttering of feet.

"Shhh," Rick whispered, "Listen!"

As we all huddled together, we held our breath, listening to a strange noise that was coming so near to our door. It sounded like a small army of sorts, feet scampering and moving quickly.

"What is that?" Rachel asked with alarm.

Before I could answer her back a charge began, and thousands and thousands of spiders began to pour into the room from under the doorway, scampering all over the walls and onto the ceiling! We all let out terrifying screams. We were all petrified of spiders! Rick was determined to save us from this predicament and focused his energies on what to do about it. He tried at first to swat the bugs but found that to be useless. There were so many of them and more just kept coming in one right after the other.

I tried to begin an Ave, but the sight of these creatures was so repulsive that I couldn't continue. Daniel rose up seeing us all struggling with fear and began to help his father in his efforts to swat at the bugs. Ricky rose up next but the more they tried to get rid of the critters the more they came from under the doorway. They were surrounding us, and driving us to huddle close with fear. I thought Rachel would die of fright when suddenly I realized these horrid spiders were not crawling on any of us! They were all about the pantry on the cans, on the shelves, crawling along the ceiling, up the walls, across the floors, but somehow they couldn't crawl on any of us.

I began to wonder if the "elect" were to be spared from harm in some supernatural way. Had all our prayers been answered? Was there an angel protecting us, standing nearby? I looked over to Rick who suddenly stopped swatting the bugs and looked back at me too. He realized the same thought I was having and noticed the bugs were keeping a close distance.

"Let God arise, and let His enemies be scattered, and let them that hate Him flee from before His face!"

Rick stood up tall in the midst of us.

I had my face half buried in Rachel's shoulder and half watching what was happening. At the sound of that psalm the bugs began to take a hurried flight from the room! Rick repeated the psalm with more vigor and in a great dignified posture.

"Let God arise, and let His enemies be scattered, and let them that hate Him flee from before His face!"

I quickly opened the Bible to that psalm.

"Here it is," I began, "Psalm 67: As smoke vanisheth, so let them vanish away: as wax melteth before the fire, so let the wicked perish at the presence of God. And let the just feast, and rejoice before God, and be delighted with gladness . . ."

It was working. The spiders were hurrying to leave our room at once. As they hurried back under the doorway, I rose up rapidly and took the jug of holy water sprinkling it on the last remaining bugs. They seemed to disappear instantly into small mists of vapor which extinguished them completely.

We all nervously laughed letting out our anxieties and stress.

"It worked mommy!" Rachel hugged me close. She started to cry now that it was all over.

"It's not over yet!" came that loud gruffy rude voice again. As I held Rachel close to me and rocked her gently in my arms, I could feel hot breath upon the back of my neck as if the devil was right behind me.

I broke out with another psalm, "Praise ye the Lord in His holy places: praise Him in the firmament of His power! Praise Him for His mighty deeds: praise Him according to the multitude of His greatness! Praise Him with sound of trumpet: praise Him with psaltery and harp! Praise Him with timbrel and chorus: praise Him with strings and organ! Praise Him on sweet—sounding cymbals; praise Him on cymbals of joy: let every spirit praise the Lord!" to which the hot breath huffed off leaving me to wipe away the perspiration on the back of my neck.

Joanne and John had their hands full as well. As they huddled together in prayer, they could hear the devils convene right outside their door and all around them. There were legions of demons of all types waiting for the chance to snatch up their souls! It wasn't made clear to John and Joanne but there were countless silent demons waiting beside more avenging spirits as well. These silent enemies were seemingly from the lower ranks of hell, and they possessed no strength or aggressive powers. These demons seemed to be confused and made sounds to mock the confusion which terrified this poor little family all the more.

John listened curiously to everything that was going on outside but he wasn't able to make out anything distinguishable from those inferior foes. Now and then these creatures would let out great moaning sounds or beast like howling for the sake of being recognized.

The avenging spirits, on the other hand, were more violent and wild. You could feel the hatred they possessed. Though they couldn't readily be seen their very presence suggested they were quite ugly and animal-like. They were like fierce warriors eager for battle, full of meanness and deception, trickery and falsehood, hatred and anger. They charged relentlessly at the door, taking turns in an odd sort of way, climbing over and on top of each other, each believing they would succeed in breaking the door to bits!

With each blow came dreadful cries of defeat and punishment from a higher authority for not being successful.

But John wasn't about to let their brutalities upset his family for long.

"What else did Jill tell you we can do?" John looked tenderly at his wife.

His gaze, so full of love, gave strength to Joanne who was faltering with fear.

"She said we should have recourse to the Blessed Mother," she got up and pointed to the brand new blessed statue. "There She is! Look at Her!" Joanne told them. "Jill once told me a beautiful story about Mary from the night of the nativity of our Lord. She told me after the Holy Family had been turned out of all the inns they came across a cave. This place was so deplorable and held in such great contempt that no one would degrade themselves to make use of it for lodging. But holy Mary and Saint Joseph did . . ."

Hearing the humility of Mary and of Saint Joseph there came a great rush of winds and footsteps stampeding at once to run far from outside John and Joanne's door. The demons despise humility and could not stand to hear the sweet story of the nativity of the King of Kings. They also feared Saint Joseph so dreadfully that they took no chances. They were fearful St. Joseph might arrive at any moment, hearing Joanne and John's meek pleas to him, to come with some much needed assistance. The serpents fled the scene at once.

"And she said Mary and Joseph were accompanied by 10,000 angels who guarded them and helped to clean and prepare this holy site for the birth of Jesus . . ."

Chapter 9

"I confess to Almighty God, and to you my brothers and sisters, that I have sinned exceedingly, through my fault, through my fault, through my most grievous fault . . ." the Sullivan family prayed together.

Each of them were earnest in their prayers, all but James, who was preoccupied with what was happening outside. Still, even though the Sullivan's couldn't tell that it was evening outside, they knew it was getting late and they were all becoming quite tired. The demons sensing this became overly excited with a renewed hope of catching one or all of them off guard.

"We have to rest," Mr. Sullivan looked over his weary family.

They had fought the good fight for so long now. The candles were burning lower and some of the wax had evaporated. It was time to try and sleep. But who could sleep with all the noise going on and the relentless battle of the evil foes?

"We'll sleep in shifts," he proposed.

"Sleep?" an evil shout sounded through the door. "You're joking, right? You'll sleep in hell before we allow you to rest! Stay up! Stay awake! You haven't earned the right to sleep!"

Mr. Sullivan completely ignored the threats and warnings being shouted at him.

"Chris, you and Patrick take Jimmy and go to the far side of the room. Colleen and Mary Alice stay here with your mother. Edward, you're to stay with me. We'll take turns reading aloud. Should one of us doze off, the other will continue reading, until it's time to wake the next shift to relieve us. All of you sleep on the floor in outstretched positions, prostrating even in your sleep and praying until you fall asleep. Though I doubt you will get much rest, nonetheless you will need some down time to rejuvenate."

There was an explosion of garbling outside the door. Some of the demons were furious at the thought of the Sullivan's resting while they were eagerly awaiting the opportunity to tear them to pieces. Other evil spirits were more cunning and better planners, lying in wait and busy preparing the snare in which to trap them in. With all of hell pitted against itself turmoil erupted.

"Let them slumber!" came the voice of a snide more cunning devil.

"Yes, let them sleep."

No one knew the evil plan this demon was conspiring to do as he encouraged the weary spiritual wayfarers to take their rest.

Mr. Sullivan ignored all of the demons wiping his brow from stress and took his leave in a chair near the door, "Bring us a candle here Eddie, and come sit down by my side."

Each of the other Sullivans blessed themselves and taking gulps of holy water said their nightly prayers before they retired to sleep. The pounding continued at the door and then it seemed to subside for a while as they fell asleep.

As soon as they all seemed peaceful in slumber the pounding commenced again, suddenly and with great force! It was apparent the evil ones wanted them to think they were not truly safe nor was it going to remain peaceful for any great length of time.

Mr. Sullivan continued with his reading, Romans 8: 35-39: "Who shall separate us from the love of Christ? Shall tribulation, or distress, or persecution, or hunger, or nakedness, or danger, or the sword? Even as it is written, 'For thy sake we are put to death all the day long. We are regarded as sheep before the slaughter.' But in all these things we overcome because of him who has loved us. For I am sure that neither death, nor life, nor angels, nor principalities, nor things present, nor things to come, nor powers, nor height, nor depth, nor any other creature will be able to separate us from the love of God, which is in Christ Jesus our Lord."

The others reclined and prostrated themselves like crosses in order to continue praying unceasingly even while they were resting. The children were exhausted soon giving in to their unyielding bodies to stay awake. They quickly fell asleep.

Mrs. Sullivan was weary too, but she fought to stay awake in spite of her exhaustion. She felt a strong need to check her children and make sure they were all safe. She was scared to her core at the hideous nonstop noises that kept emanating from behind that locked door. She knew danger wasn't far off and she feared going to sleep lest that danger found some way to enter their room.

Chris stirred and moaned a little while he slept. He was dreaming. But even in sleep there was no escaping the horrors of hell. Chris was having a nightmare. He was dreaming of being lost in a wooded area nearby to where they lived. It was dark and the limbs of the trees seemed to stretch out to grab

him and hold him prisoner. He ran from something chasing
him, though he couldn't see what or who it was. There was only
that sound of an eerie and sickening music, a soft unsettling
humming, a call in a whisper of his name. He knew he had
to run!

He came to a clearing and a large house, a mansion of
sorts. A strange mist or eerie fog seemed to ensue from the
surrounding grounds. Though the house looked foreboding
he ran up to the front door and let himself in. There was a
great eeriness inside and a strange feeling of some alarming
other presence. He made his way through the great entrance
and the foyer as someone or something beckoned him to
come upstairs. He hesitated sensing a feeling of doom until
his curiosity got the better of him. He began to mount the
staircase.

Higher and higher he rose until he found himself on the
landing at the top of the stairs. There was a door to his right.
Someone was inside that room. He slowly edged his way to the
door and putting his ear to it, gave a listen, before he tried the
doorknob to open it. The knob made a scratching sound and
the door creaked as he opened it to peer in . . .

Startled he awoke from this dream seeing in reality the
door to their own room was ajar and there was a scratching
sound as of demons wanting to make their way in. He leapt to
his feet at once and made way for the opening door, slamming
it hard on the claws of the wicked foes that desired so intensely
to gain entrance. Everyone woke with a start!

Mr. Sullivan who had dozed from his reading perked up
at once.

"Nice work, Chris! Give it some more holy water," he
congratulated his son for his swift move in closing the opening
door and had Ed hand him the bottle of holy water. Then
looking back to his book continued to find something of worth
to recite and meditate upon, "Now where was I?"

In no time at all Mr. Sullivan, fumbling with the Old
Testament, came upon Jeremias 1:19, "They will fight against

you; but they shall not prevail against you, for I am with you, says the Lord, to deliver you."

The weary old man paused for a moment letting the words sink in, "Yes, it's written right here, they shall not prevail . . ."

Upon reading this Mr. Sullivan began once again to doze off in an exhausted accidental sleep. His son Eddie also fell asleep at his knees. There was a deadening silence, an eerie stillness, like no other before. Each of the Sullivans was lost in a dream. Some stirred, while the others moaned a little. They were having nightmares, each of them. There was no rest for the wicked or the weary.

Jimmy was dreaming about playing baseball. He was up at bat. The pitch came in. He tipped it. Foul ball! The pitcher warmed up for another pitch. He threw it. Strike! Jimmy pushed the dust off of home plate with his shoe. He raised his bat over his shoulder getting ready for the next pitch. Ball two!

"Come on, come on," he was thinking.

Another pitch crossed over the plate. Strike two! The pressure was on. He needed to hit this one. The pitch looked good. BAM!

Hearing the ball crack the bat woke Jimmy from his dream. It sounded so real. Or was it a bump from the door to their room?

"Jimmy!" came a soft whisper. It sounded like Jimmy's best friend Drew.

Jimmy stirred a little trying to regain his senses from just waking up. He looked around the room. Everyone was asleep. The whisper continued again trying to catch Jimmy's attention.

"Jimmy! Let's finish our game."

The sound of Drew's voice beckoned him to come outside.

Jimmy was anxious to see where the ball had soared off to.

"Did I hit it out of the park?" he asked wiping the sleep from his eyes.

"Shhh, quiet! You don't want to wake everyone up!" the whisper coaxed him.

Jimmy got up very quietly from his corner of the room. He listened to his friend and made his way carefully and cautiously across the room to the door.

"That's right Jimmy, turn the knob very quietly. You're almost here," the whisper voice continued to coax him.

Jimmy hesitated. He wondered about all the things his dad had said. He wondered about the *Three Days of Darkness*. He wondered if he should really go outside. Was the ordeal over? How could his friend be out there? He sounded all right. He slowly convinced himself it was fine to go outside. He continued to turn the knob, believing his friend was waiting for him and ready to run off to play.

Jimmy opened the door and saw outside!

"No!" Mr. Sullivan woke up at once, "Jimmy! No!"

But it was too late. Chris was up on his feet running to close the door. But Jimmy had collapsed dead to the floor and was being dragged outside into the darkness. Chris tried to hold on to his brother's feet.

"Jimmy!" Mrs. Sullivan screamed.

There was no way to save him. A terrible and horrible laughter sounded and resounded in the air. The demons mocked their cries.

"Jimmy! No! Jimmy! No! Ha ha ha ha ha! Who'll be next?" the evil ones taunted the family.

Mrs. Sullivan was beside herself. She had to be restrained from wanting to rush outside and save her poor little boy. But Mr. Sullivan held her back rocking her and crying too as he held her in his arms.

"Who is like unto God?" she tearfully cried out loud.

Margaret Nelson was tired as well. She was reading a story about the Blessed Mother's life to Don as he nodded off to sleep in his easy chair. Seeing him struggling to stay awake Margaret covered him in a blanket and snuggled close by him. She didn't want to close her eyes fearing the demons would do something frightful.

Don jumped in his chair hearing a loud bang outside their door! It sounded like a clap of thunder right under their roof! Margaret was shaking with fear.

"What in the world?" Don muttered shifting in his seat.

There was no stopping the noise and the chaos that kept reoccurring. The evil ones were restless and it seemed they were being tortured not having stolen any new souls lately. They were anxious to fill hell with the stupid souls of mortal men, or better still, to fill hell with those who would listen to their counsel and fall by sin! They howled in anguish right outside the door, pushing and shoving one another to be heard and frighten those two poor souls inside. Each time they released their growls and cries into the air they were beaten as though they had failed in not being frightful enough. A terrible voice of great strength and magnitude could be heard scolding them and hitting them with what sounded like a strong whip or a large stick.

"Poor, poor miserable souls!" the liar began sarcastically to shout through the locked door. "You shall never rest! You are going to die! You are coming to hell! And in hell there is no hope for rest!"

"Shall I continue to read?" Margaret asked her husband, not waiting for his reply. She opened her book regarding the Blessed Mother and turned to the pages where Mary was present at the crucifixion of Jesus. "This is interesting Don. Listen to this . . ."

The demons became enraged at her soft words and the story she was unfolding. There had been great tortures at the foot of the Cross for the devils while they were forced to witness the death of the King of Kings.

Margaret carefully opened the pages and continued to read in earnest what took place on Golgotha, "Lucifer and his infernal hosts were so overwhelmed with pains and torments by the presence of the Lord and his blessed Mother, and with the fear of their impending ruin, that they would have felt greatly relieved to be allowed to cast themselves into the darkness of hell. As this was not permitted them, they fell upon one another and furiously fought with each other like hornets disturbed in their nest, or like a brood of vermin confusedly seeking some dark shelter. But their rabid fury was not that of animals, but that of demons more cruel than dragons. Then the haughty pride of Lucifer saw itself entirely vanquished and all his proud thoughts of setting his throne above the stars of heaven and drinking dry the waters of the Jordan put to shame. How weak and annihilated now was he, who so often had presumed to overturn the whole earth!"

"Stop it! Stop it at once, I say!" grueling voices could be heard from outside their door.

"How downcast and confounded he, who had deceived so many souls by false promises and vain threats!" Margaret stopped and looked around before continuing, "From now on, Lucifer, I know that thy arrogance and pride is much greater than thy strength."

A great wind as of that like an impending storm whirled about the room while great claps of thunder resounded outside the door. Great moans and frightful sounds of agonies ensued as it appeared thousands of demons were hurrying to escape being at that doorway or trying to escape with great haste at the impending tremendous footsteps of some new unwelcome visitor making his presence known.

"Who is like unto God?" Margaret froze in her place petrified with fear!

Don grabbed hold of her, trembling as well, "What is the other psalm they flee hearing?"

Margaret was too afraid to answer him.

"Continue with your reading!" Don yelled at her.

Margaret fumbled with the pages. She could barely hold the book still as she shook with great fear. The wind roared and pounded like that of a great cyclone. There was a sound like that of many being trampled. The demons were trying to hurry away. Don and Margaret wondered at their excitement what was happening.

"Read, Margaret! It is imperative that you continue to read!" Don chided her.

"This chapter deals with the demons at the foot of the Cross forced to witness the triumph of the Lord and His plan for men's redemption. It tells how these dragons were seized with inexpressible fury and how their arrogance beyond all other torments had been vanquished. It tells how they raged against themselves like blood thirsty lions to try to over take the Blessed Mother who so obediently stood at the foot of the Cross. But they were quite helpless at this most holy of all sites."

"Read Margaret, read!" Don grabbed the book and held it up for her.

Shaking with fear Margaret continued, "The fifth word of Christ from the Cross was 'I thirst'. This confirmed His triumph over the devil and his followers; the demons were filled with wrath and fury because the Lord clearly let them see their total overthrow. By these words they understood Him to say to them: If what I suffer for men and my love for them seem great to you, be assured that my love for them is still unsatiated, that it continues to long for their eternal salvation, and that the mighty waters of torments and sufferings have not extinguished it. Much more would I suffer for them, if it were necessary, in order to deliver them from your tyranny and make them powerful and strong against your malice and pride."

A great howl as if to announce a great leader crackled through the tension filled room where they were. The Nelson's huddled in the most profound fear they had ever known.

Mr. Nelson whispered, "Read, Margaret."

"At the pronouncing of the seventh word: 'Father, into Thy hands I commend My spirit!' Lucifer and all the evil spirits

instantly were allowed to depart that most holy place and
fled furiously to the deepest dungeons of hell more violently
and more suddenly than a flash of light through the riven
clouds."

"You will stop with your reading this instant!" came the
most furious and frightening voice they had ever heard in all
their lives.

The Nelson's shook with fear. Margaret fainted. Don
quickly tried to revive her. He shook her trying to awaken
her. But it was of no use. Then he realized he had to continue
reading. He was left to fumble with the book and try to take
up where his wife had left off. He wasn't sure if Margaret
would come to if he drove the evil foes away. All he knew was
that they had to continue in their defense. He had to keep
reading. Mr. Nelson scrambled to find where his wife had left
off in her reading.

"Here we go," he muttered, finding the place where Lucifer
and his demons had just been cast to the lowest regions of
hell, which is in the middle of the earth and farthest removed
from its surface.

They had been sent there in vanquish because of their
insidious acts related to the crucifixion. Once they were back
in hell they convened together in council to plot out another
downfall for the ruination of mankind.

"'Is it possible that the human nature, so inferior to my
own, shall be exalted above all the creatures!' Lucifer began.
'From the beginning I have held this humanity as my greatest
enemy; it has always filled me with intolerable abhorrence.
O men, so favored and gifted by your God, whom I abhor,
and so ardently loved by Him! How shall I hinder your good
fortune? How shall I bring upon you my unhappiness, since
I cannot destroy the existence you have received? What shall
we now begin, O my followers? How shall we restore our
reign? How shall we recover our power over men? How shall
we overcome them?'"

An evil laugh came forth from someone who was listening at the doorway. Mr. Nelson froze with terror thinking who it might be lying in wait for him with some foul trap.

"You think that book will be your protection against the wrath that I have in store for you and your wife?" an angry powerful voice set forth. "You arrogant little man! Who do you think *you* are in the presence of the King of Darkness?"

Mr. Nelson gave no reply. He sat there huddled with his unconscious wife sweating in fear and anxiety. He wondered how he could escape the snare this cunning serpent was devising. With all his courage, Mr. Nelson read further, unleashing an even greater racket outside his door.

He read silently and from that book he uncovered the following:

"'Come all of ye to take counsel what we are to do; for I desire to hear your opinions,' Lucifer announced to his pitiful subjects."

Don surmised from his reading that hell was convening to plot out how they would destroy mankind just as they were presently trying to do. They have always been relentless in their attempts to bring about mankind's ruination.

"Some of the devils charged themselves with perverting the inclinations of children at their conception and birth; others to induce parents to be negligent in their education and instruction of their children, either through an inordinate love or aversion, and to cause a hatred of parents among the children. Some offered to create hatred between husbands and wives, to place them in the way of adultery, or to think little of the fidelity promised to their conjugal partners. All agreed to sow among men the seeds of discord, hatred and vengeance, proud and sensual thoughts, desire of riches or honors, and by suggesting sophistical reasons against all the virtues Christ has taught; above all they intended to weaken the remembrance of His Passion and Death, of the means of salvation, and of the eternal pains of hell. By these means the demons hoped to burden all the powers and the faculties of men with solicitude for earthly affairs and sensual pleasures, leaving them little time for spiritual thoughts and their own salvation."

"Lucifer heard these different suggestions and answered them saying, 'I am much beholden to you for your opinions: I approve of them and adopt them all; it will be easy to put them into practice with those, who do not profess the law given by this Redeemer to men, though with those who accept and embrace these laws, it will be a difficult enterprise. But against this law and against those that follow it, I intend to direct all my wrath and fury and I shall most bitterly persecute those who hear the doctrine of this Redeemer and become His disciples; against these must our most restless battle be waged to the end of the world . . .'"

At those words a ravaging fury of pounds and threats could be heard nearly breaking the door down.

"Do you think that by reading our plans you will know how we will attack and conquer you? Stupid little man! You have not the great intelligence of angels. Nor do you comprehend the nature we devise in our own contempts of you! Ignorant man! We shall gobble you up and spit you out! Woe to you who think you can withstand us!"

After the serpent finished speaking, terrible sounds of anguish and tortures could be heard, as if Lucifer was taking his wrath out upon his own followers, fearing that he might fail to corrupt this obstinate man who read the stories of the Blessed Mother for guidance and Her instruction. The noises seemed to be going away from where they had begun. The demons were planning a new course of attack. And just when Mr. Nelson should have been praying and reading the most, he swooned from his tiredness and fell fast asleep.

It didn't take long at all before Margaret awoke with a start at the quietness that was surrounding them. She wondered at the stillness. She looked at the blessed candle that had burned so low. She wondered what time it was or how many days had passed. It had seemed like they had been shut up in that room for ages. Maybe it was over now. Maybe they could resume their lives and forget about the terrors that had plagued them for so long.

"Margaret!" came a familiar voice at the door.

Margaret perked her head up to listen more keenly.

"Clare is that you?" she tearfully whispered back.

"Yes Margaret, please let me in. I've come such a long way and I want so much to see you again. I miss you, my darling. Please let me come in. I must see you once more."

"Clare!" Margaret's heart nearly broke for joy. "Oh, my dearest Clare!"

She rose at once and headed straight for the door, disregarding every warning not to look outside and reckless to see her beloved family member once again at any cost.

"Come to me, Margaret. I've missed you so. I must tell you a great secret. Come, my sweet Margaret. I'm waiting here for you."

"Coming, my darling," Margaret whispered so as not to really be heard.

Then she quietly tiptoed over to the locked door picking up the blessed candle to make her way through the darkness. Upon reaching the door she quietly turned the knob.

"Oh Clare, I've missed you . . . you have no idea . . ." Margaret's words left off.

There was no time to scream. There was no time to shut the door back to its closed position. It was too late. Margaret had looked outside! Clare was not behind the door. Margaret had been caught in the carefully thought out snare of the devil. Dropping the blessed candle from her hand, she fell to the floor and died instantly!

Immediately a great howling sound shook the house and a gleeful victory was heard, "We're going to get you next!"

Mr. Nelson awoke with a start hearing his foes shout this out to him. Seeing the blessed candle lying on its side, next to his collapsed wife on the floor, he shouted, "No! No, Margaret! What have you done? Oh my God, what have you done?"

Somehow he managed to make his way across the room to close the door without looking out. Then he cuddled his lifeless wife in his arms and rocking her gently he began to lament.

Chapter 10

I am not sure how, but by the grace of God, we managed somehow to make it through the first day and night. There was still another day and night to go and then if we were lucky there was the third and final day. On that final day, the ordeal would be over. The promise of sunshine and a new more holy way of life was in store.

"Please Lord," I prayed, "help all of us to make it."

But for the present there was no time to sit idle. Everything was in constant turmoil. The demons were relentless in their efforts to frighten us and determined to trap any soul foolish enough to be lured into one of their carefully laid snares. The children seemed to suffer most, petrified at every howl and disturbance they heard. They were tried and worn out. We were all worn out. But there was no time to reflect upon what could have been or should have been. There was only the relentless offering of prayers, psalms and hymns. The only way to come through it all was to keep the faith and persevere onward. Baby Kate was crying. It was so hard for her to sleep. Her whole routine had been thrown off course. So between the crying and the constant noise going on outside our patience was beginning to wear a little thin. I tried to rock the baby in one arm and held on to my trembling Rachel in the other. Rick was huddled with the boys as we sang out in weary voices, "Onward Christian Soldiers!" But it was no use.

It suddenly got very quiet. That frightened us most of all. Whenever the stillness came a great new episode of some terrible ordeal was sure to follow. It was no different this day. We stopped what we were all doing to have a listen, which was probably the worst thing we could have done. We should have been more diligent in our prayers. Nonetheless, we strained to see if we could hear something out there in the darkness.

There was nothing, no sounds, no whisperings. One could almost determine the devils had fled and we were finally left alone to resume life the way it should be lived. Ricky sat up straight to have a good listen.

"They've gone, mommy! I think it's over!" he was so hopeful. We were all hopeful.

"Listen!" Rick's ears were far better than mine.

I strained trying to listen. Very softy, barely noticeable at first, I began to hear the sounds of birds singing in the distance. It sounded like a great deal of birds. They were not sounds of alarm, but of singing, chirping happily and such. It was refreshing and a welcoming sound, one that we had missed so terribly while we were being pounded by great throngs of ominous warnings and frightful howls from the depths of hell.

"It's over!" Daniel sat up smiling.

"Wait a minute," Rick hesitated. He was leery of what might be happening.

"Let us pray!" I reminded everyone to keep vigilant.

"No mommy, listen. Don't you hear the birds?" Rachel spoke softly.

"Yes, I know baby. I do hear them, but we must continue with our prayers," I tried to warn her.

The room we were in became very still. It was unnervingly still. It was as if a great storm was about to hit with full force at any minute. We all braced for that turmoil to happen. But nothing did. There was a soft but soothing music that could be heard as well. It was so refreshing. It lured us into a false sense of security and hope. We delighted in it, forgetful of the dangers.

Then without any further warning the flame on the blessed candle seemed to lessen.

"Look at the candle!" Daniel shouted to all of us.

Rick was terribly afraid the small flame was going to go out, when I reminded him it could not be extinguished in the houses of the elect. Suddenly a small midst or vapor, like that of a small cloud, rose just above the candle and started to rise still higher in the little room. All eyes were upon it, watching to see what would happen next. As the cloud began to rise it became larger in size. A strange light began to emanate from it casting an eerie glow about the room. I held Rachel tightly to myself as we all became transfixed.

Then from the center of this illumination came a form, hard to make out at first, but slowly transfiguring into the most beautiful woman we had ever seen.

"Look mommy, it's Mary!" Rachel smiled. For the first time since the ordeal had taken place the child was not afraid.

The figure of this lady was hard to determine. It wasn't clear. But one could make out the features of a woman clothed in a blue mantle over her head and a white gown cinched at the waist with a golden belt. There was a small glowing circle about her head somewhat like that of a halo. Her arms were outstretched at her sides, like those of our statute and how most paintings depicted Mary to stand. She was majestic in figure and alluring in nature. We all continued to stare waiting to see what she was going to do. But she did nothing for some time. She was watching us, as if she was studying us. She was smiling on us and we smiled back at her. Then without warning she began to speak.

"My dear children, you have been patient for so long now. I am most pleased with you. More importantly, Our Lord is most pleased with you as well. That is why I have come here today. I have come to inform you that because you have been so faithful in your endeavors the Lord has granted the petitions heard to shorten the *Three Days of Darkness*. A fearful battle has ensued and the Lord is victorious. Legions of demons have been cast back into hell. The earth will be calm now and a renewed sense of faith will be established . . ."

She continued speaking with a very calming voice, a very gentle voice, a very soothing voice. We all were quite taken in by her charm and beauty. She was a lovely figure of a lady. I couldn't help studying her as well. The children were immediately drawn in by her presence and they sat attentively listening to every word of her message. I noticed Rick was also taken in by her demeanor. As she continued to speak the room began to filter with air that smelled like those of roses. This was a smell often associated with the presence of the Queen of Heaven. It was refreshing after having endured the stench of rottenness for so long now.

We were all eager to resume a peaceful way of life once again. I was wondering what it would be like outside. Suddenly it occurred to me there may be many corpses everywhere. If so, who would help bury the dead? Or was it beautiful outside? Were the birds really singing happily again? Was the sun shining brightly in the bluest of skies? Would we find our neighbors refreshed and strengthened in their faith?

The lady continued, "This battle was a fierce one between the Almighty and Satan and his followers. It has been a long time coming. The Lord saw a need to do battle now. Many wicked people have been lost. Many would not believe in the warnings of the Lord. But you have persevered and believed. You are chosen. It has been families like yours that have become most pleasing to the Lord. He has heard your prayers. He has sent His angels to guard you through this time of great troubles . . ."

As Mary continued to speak, I suddenly became a little uneasy. It was hard to explain at first. I couldn't quite put my finger on it. Something just didn't sit well with me. Something about her didn't feel right. Call it woman's intuition or whatever you will, but something felt very disturbing to me. Nonetheless, I continued to listen to her.

"My children, you have done everything the good Lord asked of you. You have fought the good fight. You have constantly prayed. Now is the time to reward you for all your troubles. Now is the time to show you paradise on earth. Behold, the earth has been purified for the elect. Come with me and see the land that has been so carefully prepared for you . . ."

She pointed with an outstretched arm to the door. She wanted us to open it and go outside. We were ready to go, all of us. It had seemed like we were cooped up for such a long time. We were ready to stretch our limbs and breathe some new fresh air. We got up from our sitting and kneeling positions on the floor. We brushed ourselves off. The children were very excited. Daniel was in the lead. Ricky came in a close second. Rachel was standing by me.

As I picked up baby Kate I glanced over at the still slowly burning blessed candle. I noticed it was only one third burnt down. Three days couldn't have possibly passed by us yet. I looked to the locked door. Daniel was getting ready to open it. I glanced down to the floor beneath the door. There was no light shining in. If it was bright and sunny outside there would have been light shining in from under the doorway!

"Stop!" I screamed to the boys. "Don't touch that door!"

In a swift motion and with precise accuracy I swooped down and picked up the jug of holy water. Opening the top of it as quickly as I could I flung some of that precious water at the apparition. In an instant great screams could be heard like those that come forth from a great agony. "You cursed brat! You little . . . We'll be back. Next time you won't be as lucky!" The figure trailed off disappearing into a vapor, like a cloud of smoke.

A clamor of terrible sounds ensued from out there in the darkness, terrible sounds of great lamenting and agonies. The sounds of tortures and stampeding, or running to get away from a tormentor, could be heard among the sounds of great cries to frighten and great cries of intense pains.

The children were speechless, standing near the door and looking down to the floor beneath the door.

"How did you know?" Rick asked me.

"I was feeling strange listening to her. Then I noticed there was no light coming from under the doorway. The candle hadn't burned down far enough for three days yet. We still have a ways to go. Come back here boys. Get on your knees and be thankful we didn't go out or look outside that door."

Kate began to cry with all the racket going on around us. So I continued to rock her as gently as I could with one arm and held on to my trembling Rachel with the other.

༄

John and Joanne were not doing much better. They had scarcely gotten any sleep from the night before. Jess was petrified at every haunting sound. And the turmoil was relentless as if a great wrecking crew was pulverizing the house bit by bit. The great darkness that filled the room, except for the little flame from the blessed candle, was oppressive. No one had ever seen such pitch blackness before these three days of so much terror. Nonetheless, they continued to pray and persevered in pious hymns and conversations.

The noise outside suddenly stopped. There was an uneasy feeling of doom that filled the room. Jess sat upright to give a better listen to what was happening. Joanne put her arms around her terrified daughter. John looked up from praying in a prostrate position on the floor. The sound of many small feet scurrying all about the house and the door could softly be heard. At first it sounded like a few feet pattering. But soon the noise grew to what seemed like thousands of clawed feet hurrying about.

The doorknob of the door to their room began to turn. Someone was trying to gain entrance into the room! All eyes were upon the door! Not being able to open it, the unwelcomed visitor began to push at the door. Jess and Joanne watched in horror as the top portion of the door and the bottom section began to bend in and out as if the door itself were breathing! As it bent it seemed to stretch to the limits. John feared it would splinter and break under such pressure. He immediately ran for the holy water to douse the door with it. As soon as the water touched the door a steam like vapor rose to the ceiling. But in spite of John's efforts to secure the door, the demon's efforts to open it and get inside continued.

"Let God arise, and let His enemies be scattered, and let them that hate Him flee from before His Face!" John protested.

Joanne scrambled to find their Bible and joined in with John adding to the verse, "As smoke vanisheth, so let them vanish away: as wax melteth before the fire, so let the wicked perish at the presence of God." Then seeing Jess so very frightened, Joanne handed the holy book to her and pressed her to continue reading.

Jess shuttered at first, but continued to read, "And let the just feast, and rejoice before God: and be delighted with gladness." The reading gave Jess new confidence and so they all joined in together praying the rest of the psalm aloud.

"Sing ye to God, sing a psalm to His name, make way for Him who ascendeth upon the west: the Lord is His name."

"Rejoice ye before Him: but the wicked shall be troubled at His presence, who is the father of orphans, and the judge of widows." . . .

As they all persisted in reading, the great bending of the door began to subside. The enemy was defeated and they could hear him reluctantly go away. Great whisperings could be heard, as if huge beasts were huddled together devising some sort of new plan to gain entrance to their room.

Joanne broke out in song as she kept focused on the new statue of the Blessed Mother she had just recently bought. Jess followed her mother's lead, courageously echoing her mother's hymn. John joined in their efforts and continued until they had sung every verse.

As quickly as they finished one defense, the frightened little family picked right back up with a new one. Joanne grabbed for the rosary and blessed herself to begin, "In the name of the Father, and of the Son and of the Holy Ghost Amen . . ."

John got back on the floor prostrating, since this seemed to be the best position to pray in. It showed great humiliation and the demons hated to be overcome by such humbleness. Jess sat close to her mother as Joanne reached her arms around her daughter and prayed the prayers while she encircled her.

But they were hungry and tired. It had been a grueling day and night. There was still another day or night to go. And if they were lucky, perhaps they'd only have to endure a partial third day. Joanne began to weep at how trying every minute had become. She was so overwhelmed with how frightened Jess was besides her own great fears. The battles were relentless and there was no time for any peace or real rest. The chaos continued uninterrupted.

John was frightened too. His prayers were contrite and sorrowful begging God to be merciful to them. It was a frightful agony to think he could have been left outside in that darkness. He kept remembering almost being caught up in the darkness when it had just begun. And so, he was grateful to God for sparing him and allowing him to get back inside with his family once again.

He shuttered as he remembered driving to work. The sky above him was slowly becoming black at the horizons. It was as if black ink was being poured and it flowed like water along the horizons. Slowly, steadily, inch by inch, it covered the early morning skies. Cars were stopped to view this strange phenomenon. People were standing around pointing at the sky. Traffic was snarled and horns were honking.

He too had stopped to view the sky. It was mysterious and alluring. People were caught up in wonder when suddenly John realized the danger. How many others knew of the impending dangers? He wondered how many were aware of the *Three Days of Darkness*. He knew in an instant he had to try and get right home!

He tried to make a U-turn right there on the boulevard, right in the middle of traffic. Then he floored it going in the opposite direction. By the time he reached his driveway, the sky was nearly totally black! The automatic garage door went up. It was the last bit of electrical power he would see working. He was able to get into the garage. Then it went totally black! He closed his eyes immediately! Frightened, he would be lost forever, he felt his way as quickly as he could to the locked door. He knew his wife and daughter would be waiting on the other side. He had to get to them.

Far in the distance he could hear a great commotion of people screaming, horns blaring, and the sounds anyone would hear on an ordinary day. But it was no ordinary day. The screaming subsided. The horns just ceased. There were no sounds from birds. There was no sound from crickets. There were no sounds from anything. There was only an ominous stillness forewarning a terrible chastisement about to befall mankind.

And he was frantic that it had already begun. He wondered if Joanne would open the door for him. He struggled with the lock and banged on the door. He could hear his wife and daughter talking, wondering if they should open the door.

Then in the distance, he could hear a strange and horrifying sound. Hell had been opened and legions of demons were being released. He wondered if he would make it inside before they had a chance to find him.

He called out to Joanne, "Please, open the door! It's me! Please, Joanne! You have to let me in!"

Somehow, by the grace of God, the door opened and he was able to quickly jump inside without anyone seeing outside and quickly locked the door behind him. He remembered hugging his family in such a great relief that they were all safe and together. He told them what he had seen outside, how the sky had become black as if ink were being saturated all over it. He told them of the people all standing around mesmerized by the phenomenon. How foolish they had been.

"Didn't they know? Why didn't they prepare? Weren't they ever told anything about this prophecy? Why weren't they told?" he stood shaking as he held his family close to him.

"You're safe now," Joanne had told him.

And that was all that seemed to matter.

A loud pounding interrupted his chain of thoughts and a ferocious villain began to shout.

"These days are not over yet! We still have time to attack you and this dilapidated structure you call a house! We will not rest until we have taken you with us! You will come with us! You shall all die a horrid death! Time is running out for you! Die you ingrates! Die you wretched fools!"

Joanne huddled close to Jess. They were both crying. But Joanne knew they had to keep the faith and keep praying like they had been warned to do. It was the only way to retaliate and keep alive. John made his way over to them and hugged them close too. He broke down himself under the terrible stress he had been under. But his heart was filled with such love for his family it became as if a prayer unto itself. The villain at the door was disgusted by it and fled the door.

"Let's get something to eat," John suggested seeing they were so hungry and tired. "You fix something Joanne, while I keep a vigil reading about love."

John had noticed on more than one occasion that the devils went away from the door as soon as they perceived anything that had to do with love. They were filled with such vengeance and hate that they could not bear to hear or witness any such sweet sentiments. The demons used these opportunities to reassemble and devise some new strategies to plan their courses for attack.

John began with a chapter in the New Testament. "Let me begin with the fourth chapter of St. John. 'Beloved: God is love . . .'"

Great wails of terrible anguish came forth from behind the doorway. John smiled knowing he had picked a ripe verse and continued gaining strength in the Word.

"In this has the love of God been shown in our case, that God has sent His Only-begotten Son into the world that we may live through him. In this is the love, not that we have loved God, but that He has first loved us, and sent His Son a propitiation for our sins. Beloved, if God has so loved us, we also ought to love one another. No one has ever seen God. If we love one another, God abides in us and His love is perfected in us." . . .

As John continued to read Joanne reached for the can opener and began to open some tuna and canned fruit so as to make them something to eat. Jess began to relax a bit, if one could relax, so to speak. She assisted her mother getting out paper plates and plastic utensils that could be thrown away after they ate. She opened a jug of water and began to pour out glasses for all of them. She listened keenly to her father's words. The reading gave her courage.

"Here's another good one. It's from the Epistle of St. Paul to the Colossians," John had fumbled through the New Testament.

"Brethren: Put on, as God's chosen ones, holy and beloved, a heart of mercy, kindness, humility, meekness, patience. Bear with one another and forgive one another, if anyone has a grievance against any other; even as the Lord has forgiven you, so also do you forgive. But above all these things have charity, which is the bond of perfection." . . .

And with these words they sat down to eat. They said grace and Joanne picked up the Holy Book and continued to find chapters of love to read aloud as they partook of the simple meal that was laid before them.

"This is from the Epistle of St. Paul to the Romans," Joanne cleared her throat. Then in a childish playful manner she stuck her tongue out to the door, as if to spite the devil.

"Brethren: Owe no man anything except to love one another; for he who loves his neighbor has fulfilled the law. For 'You shall not commit adultery. You shall not kill. You shall not steal. You shall not bear false witness. You shall not covet'; and if there is any other commandment, it is summed up in this saying, *'You shall love your neighbor as yourself.'* Love does no evil to a neighbor. Love therefore is the fulfillment of the Law."

When they had finished with their humble meal John could see that his family was very tired. They were struggling not to go to sleep. They were frightened. But they needed this well deserved sleep so as to be able to carry on for one more day.

"I'll continue to read. I want you both to try and get some sleep. Prostrate on the floor and give an ear to me while I finish reading more about love," he instructed them.

John raised his voice so that the demons could hear him speak more about love and kept them at bay.

Joanne and Jess immediately took his advice and got down on the ground in order to pray and fall asleep. Though the poundings of hateful demons continued, this little family was so exhausted they soon fell fast asleep. John continued to read, trying to keep watch, and desiring above all else to keep everyone safe. There was no time to waste. Every second was a battle against the evil foes. But in the course of his reading the book suddenly dropped from his weary hands. He had fallen asleep.

It was a terrible danger to leave off from praying during these times. They had been warned. They didn't have the luxury of falling asleep like the apostles had that night long ago in the Garden of Gethsemane. The apostles had Jesus praying for them as a back up then. This little family had no one praying for them now.

And so, seeing their opportunity the enemy launched a quiet attack. Being spirits and able to take on any form, they squeezed their way through the keyhole and entered the room where the three unfortunate souls slept.

It was a restless sleep for those weary pilgrims. If they weren't tossing from being so uncomfortable they were tossing from the nightmares they continued to have. Joanne was particularly restless when she suddenly awoke with a start and found a dark horrid figure standing over her. She screamed waking the others. Jess awoke to find a frightful face staring directly into hers. And John jumped up for the holy water splashing it all about the room. There were dark ominous figures everywhere!

Chapter 11

Mrs. Sullivan never recovered from the loss of her beloved Jimmy. Mr. Sullivan therefore had to redouble his efforts to pray and to hold the rest of the family together. They were all very drained and weary. Mary Alice glanced over to the blessed candles burning and noticed the wax had burned down to about two thirds of the way.

"Look," she pointed out to everyone, "The candles have already burned for two days. We're approaching the third and final day of our ordeal. Please, pray to God, we survive this!"

"We can do it! I know we can do it!" Chris replied. "We'll beat those demons!"

"Sure we will now!" Mr. Sullivan joined in. "Not too much further to go!"

He hugged his sorrowful wife and made her believe in prayers and sacrifices.

"We have to continue onward, for the sake of our children," he said tearfully.

At those words Mrs. Sullivan broke down with pitiful sobs. Everyone began to cry. Hearing the sounds of their wailings the demons rejoiced with loud roars of hideous laughter. This is what they sought, to weaken the Sullivan's stronghold. Once the family began to feel dejected and sad the devils would make another move to overcome them.

Eddie looked at the locked door and saw the claws of multiple demons poking from beneath, above and through the sides of the weakened door. There were long nails and crooked fingers trying to gain entrance even through the tiniest openings. A peaceful moment never seemed to come. This enemy would not rest from their attacks and tried in every way possible to get into the room where the Sullivan's prayed, wanting to devour that grief stricken family at any moment.

"Let us pray!" Eddie screamed.

Mr. Sullivan stood tall in the midst of them, "Yes, let us pray. Let us have recourse to our heavenly Father Who will keep a watchful eye over us. Bring me the Bible, Colleen."

Obedient Colleen did as she was told, handing the Good Book over to her dad. He patted her on the head and opened the book to St. Peter 5: 6-11 and began to read aloud.

"Beloved: Humble yourselves under the mighty hand of God, that He may exalt you in the time of visitation; cast all your anxiety upon Him, because He cares for you. Be sober, be watchful! For your adversary the devil, as a roaring lion, goes about seeking someone to devour. Resist him, steadfast in the faith, knowing that the same suffering befalls your brethren all over the world. But the God of all grace, Who has called us unto His eternal glory in Christ Jesus, will Himself, after we have suffered a little while, perfect, strengthen and establish us. To Him is the glory and the dominion forever and ever."

Everyone at once said, "Amen."

The demons shrieked and let out horrifying howls in hearing that. Disturbed by the peacefulness the Sullivan's were trying to recover, the evil army of aggravators took flight to rethink a new plan of attack.

Meanwhile, Mrs. Sullivan began to think about her sorrowful behavior and suppressed her tears more earnestly. She felt more determined to assist those of her children who had been spared and she began to reflect on thoughts about her neighbors.

"Yes, what has happened to our neighbors? What have they suffered compared to us? Maybe we have been spared much more compared to what might be happening to them. Think about poor Mr. and Mrs. Nelson. Do you remember he had that problem with his leg? Maybe they never made it to shelter."

"What about Susan and Ed King? They didn't believe!"

The children gasped!

"How are Jill and Rick holding up with all those children? Can you just imagine? All over the world people are suffering at the hands of hell! People, right this moment, are dying of fright! People are being tempted just like our Jimmy was . . ."

<hr/>

"Now where was I?" Mr. Nelson struggled alone to keep his sanity. He was beside himself with grief at the loss of his dearly departed wife. But he kept vigilant and continued praying. He turned to St. John, Chapter 3, and tearfully read, "Beloved: Do not be surprised if the world hates you. We know that we have passed from death to life, because we love the brethren. He who does not love abides in death. Everyone that hates his brother is a murderer."

"And you know that no murderer has eternal life abiding in him," echoed a familiar seductive voice. It was the sound of Don's old lover Jen.

"Open the door now. There is nothing that stands between us anymore," Jen suggested.

Don was filled with hatred at hearing Jen's voice again. He began to loose his grip on reality having heard so many horrifying sounds and temptations for days. He missed his beloved Margaret who found out too late that her husband had loved another and that their love was less than she had always thought it was.

"Get away from that door!" Margaret warned the evil woman.

Who are you to tell me what to do?" Jen snapped back.

It sounded as though both Margaret and Jen were at the door.

"Margaret? Beloved, is that you?" Don cried out.

"Yes, love. It is I!" she echoed back.

"He's mine!" Jen shouted angrily. "You stay away from him!"

"You're nothing but a hussy! Don has no interest in you!" Margaret retaliated.

Don listened intently to everything going on. Suddenly there came the sound of a slap! Then another! A fight seemed to ensue from behind that locked door. Margaret could be heard struggling to overcome her assailant.

"Margaret? Margaret?" Don became frantic.

But there came no reply. Caught up in the moment Don realized his wife was in trouble and he needed to rescue her. He got up instinctively heading for the door. Every warning about not listening to what happens outside, about not opening the door, was tossed to the wind. All Don wanted to do was to see Margaret again, to help her, to hold her in his arms. He struggled with his leg as best he could, dragging his heavy foot across the floor.

"I'm coming, Margaret! Hold on! I'm coming!"

The room seemed to swirl with excitement. Don was really determined to go out there to help his wife. It took a tremendous deal of restraint on the part of the demons to hold back for just a few more seconds. Don's hand was on the door. He began to turn the knob.

"I'm coming, Margaret! Hold on! I'm coming!"

A whirlwind of winds seemed to drag Margaret off.

"I'm coming, Margaret! Please, hold on! I'm hurrying!"

And in the next instant the door to that tiny room was opened and a legion of demons devoured poor Mr. Nelson.

The days and nights were all the same, both were filled with such total darkness and the horrifying sounds of legions of demons howling and screaming everywhere! I wasn't sure how my children had survived this ordeal so far. They were trembling so for days! As much as I trusted the Lord to safeguard us, I also began to doubt we'd all ever make it through what was to come. Rick was terrified as well, you could see it in his eyes, but he kept up a brave face in order to keep the children confident things would eventually be all right.

I continued to read from my prayer book, "God is love, and he who abides in love abides in God, and God in him. In this is love perfected with us, that we may have confidence in the day of judgement; because as He is, even so are we also in this world. There is no fear in love; but perfect love casts out fear, because fear brings punishment. And he who fears is not perfected in love. Let us therefore love, because God first loved us. If anyone says, *'I love God,'* and hates his brother, he is a liar. For how can he who does not love his brother, whom he sees, love God, Whom he does not see? And this commandment we have from Him, that he who loves God should love his brother also."

Tears began to well up in my eyes. I was so afraid, not only for myself, but for Rick and our children. I was afraid for our neighbors and friends. I was afraid my faith wasn't strong enough and we wouldn't make it. I was afraid at what would be waiting for the survivors once these three terrible days had passed. What would the world be like? Would there be much to clean up? Who would bury the dead? Or would God sweep the earth clean for His elect and allow them to proceed to live the lives they were truly meant to live? Would there be peace all over the world? Would man turn his attention readily to God and love our Creator with magnanimous hearts? How would it be living off the land like our forefathers? Would it be just as hard to begin our new lives as it was to have survived the three long terribly dark days?

I thought about Father McGrath and all he had told us, all that he tried so hard to forewarn us about. In so few words he tried to convey all that we were now experiencing. Where was he now? Had he survived the turmoil? Or was he fighting with the demons and his faith just as we were? I wanted to hear him speak, wanted to see him standing before us strong and tall, leading us onward! He was such a powerful figure of a man, so rich in scripture and those things of the church. He so genuinely cared for his congregation. You could see it in his eyes.

"We'll get through this, honey," Rick said ever so gently to me.

I hadn't seen him looking at me while I was lost in deep thoughts.

"We'll be all right, mommy," Daniel interjected too.

The rest of the children joined in hugging me tightly and began to cry.

I couldn't help it. I broke down sobbing. I wasn't as confident we'd all make it. The world as we had once known it was being scourged and burned even as we sat there waiting. Fierce battles were being waged both in the spiritual realm and in the physical realm. Demons weren't only looking for our demise but were also raging war with the angels of light! There wasn't just the howls and cries of defeat being heard. There was justice and punishment being ordained. There was a new world order being structured that would bring men back to worshipping God in the way it was always meant to be.

Oh men, see how far we have strayed from our God! Look at how we are punished for the many sins of men! Look at how we have offended our Lord! Pray, yes we must pray! Even though we are tired and weary we must persevere in prayer. Now is the day when we must make up for lost time! If only we had prayed all along. If only we had watched for the signs and realized our destiny. Perhaps we could have been spared all this.

Similar thoughts and actions towards piety encircled the globe. Everyone was sorry for having offended God. Prostrating in solemn penitential fashion, poor sinners were repenting with contrite hearts, afraid it was all too late.

My thoughts turned to John and Joanne hoping they were all right and that they were surviving the punishments fairly well. I hoped so much to see them again. I thought of Mr. Nelson, hoping he was faring all right with his leg. Margaret would dote over him so. They were such a loving couple. I hoped Rick and I would have the same deep appreciation and love for one another too as we aged, if we aged, if we made it past the turmoil we were in.

Then my thoughts turned back to Father McGrath. I tried to go over in my mind everything he had told us. Were we doing everything we should be doing? Did we leave anything left undone? Where was he now when we needed him most?

I imagined the church and the rectory, so deserted, so desolate. Poor Father, I assumed, probably left there so alone. I pitied him for not having someone there to comfort and encourage him through these darkest days.

How often I was absorbed by his sermons Sunday after Sunday as he focused on loving one another and keeping us all strong in our faith. I remember his talks with tears running down his face, the earnestness in his voice, in his soul, to try and reach out to each of us with tenderness.

Whenever we called, whenever we needed him, he was there. So many had asked him to bless their homes, and he came. So many had asked for holy water, and he brought it. So many needed blessed statues, and he accommodated them.

He was a true pastor of the faith. No other church had such a gift from God than in him.

But who was comforting him now? How would he get through these most horrid of days alone? Who would help and assist him, who had helped so many others? Where would he get his courage from? Poor, poor Father McGrath. I began to sob for him, genuinely concerned for his safety. Then regaining some control of myself, I realized he was a man of the cloth, holy and righteous. If anyone knew how to combat the demons, he surely did.

Rick took the prayer book from my hands and hugged me. He began to sob as well. We all had a good cry. We needed to release the fears and anxieties we had been inundated with. As we held each other tightly, I found some consolation in a group hug.

Then without warning my eyes widened in terror. Daniel who had once seemed so brave and courageous was visibly shaken and distraught. He sat away from us loosing his grip on reality. It was easy to let go. Nothing of any semblance of normality was left. The constant clamoring of our home being torn apart and the shrieks and howls from the ungodly had taken its toll. I cried out his name. But as if lost, he did not hear me, he never responded. Rick turned to see what the matter was. We rushed to his side wondering if he had fallen asleep. There was no movement coming from him any longer.

"Daniel!" I screamed.

"Oh, my God!" Rick echoed shaking him.

It was no use. Daniel had been frightened so fiercely . . . it had all been too much for him . . . for all of us. Daniel was dead.

"He's gone," was all Rick could say to me.

"No! No! No! It isn't true! Not Daniel! Not my Daniel!" I broke into uncontrollable sobs.

The rest of the children screamed and cried as well.

The demons howled too, ecstatic another mortal had lost the fight!

"What will we do with him? We can't leave him here," Rick looked at me.

My eyes widened in terror, "You can't put him outside! No, I won't let you! You can't put my baby out there with them! No, I'll die first!" I yelled.

In the commotion I hadn't realized the toll this had taken on the rest of my children. Rachel was beginning to become dazed herself. She got up and walked over to the little car seat baby Kate was in. She started to talk softly to her little sister. Then she began to sing a little song, all the while Ricky was crying. And in this little episode of confusion, Rick was all the more determined to put Daniel's little body outside the door.

We hadn't realized in all the commotion that Rachel was poking and pulling on baby Kate but there was no response from our angel.

"Baby Kate! Baby Kate!" Rachel called out. "Look mommy, baby Kate won't wake up."

I jumped from my place at once and rushed to their side. Placing my fingers on baby Kate's neck I searched frantically for a pulse! I turned to Rick.

"This can't be! No, this isn't happening! How could this little soul be taken from us? This can't be real!" I screamed.

Rick rushed to feel the baby as well. He was shocked to find things just as I had said. Then he embraced me, "We've got to hold on! We can't loose our grip now! We have to trust God! We have to remember our faith!"

I was crying so hard I hardly heard a word he had said. In my sorrows I turned to catch the sight of Ricky standing up and walking for the door. "They must be put out!" he simply said reaching for the doorknob.

"No, no Ricky," I cried in disbelief and pleading.

In the next instant, Ricky fell to the floor. He wasn't moving! I shook my head trying to regain my senses. Then I started to emotionally break down. I could bear no more. I frantically made my way to my little boy and swept him up into my arms hugging him so tightly and rocking him, weeping and repeating over and over, "No, no, no, this just can't be."

Rick swooped low to try and catch a collapsing Rachel. Our little girl had had quite enough of demon's threats and cries that she could bear no more. She too was lifeless! In all of five minutes or so my entire family had collapsed and died before my very eyes! I went into deep shock.

"They must be put out," Rick turned to me in disbelief.

"This can't be so. It can't be so," I stammered.

"What was it Father McGrath had told us? Some children will be taken up to Heaven, to spare them the horror of these days. Jill, they're in a better place now."

"No, no, no," I just kept rocking.

Rick came over to me and took our son from my arms. I sat there watching him gather their little bodies together ready to put them outside the door. I felt helpless to move. Rick made his way back to me and held me in his arms.

"We're going to be all right," he kept saying. "We're going to be all right."

In the next instant, I awoke with a start. Rachel was holding me. Daniel was hugging Ricky and baby Kate was crying. Rick was reciting a rosary and sprinkling holy water about the room. Seems I had dozed off from exhaustion remembering the words Father had left us with, about children being taken up to Heaven beforehand.

I grabbed my children with such joy and exhilaration I could hardly contain myself! Rick came over to join in our group hug as well.

John got up to stretch his legs, while Joanne proceeded to open up some cans of food. Jess was trying to get a little sleep. All the while John stretched he prayed. Joanne was praying too. Everything they did became a prayer. They were relentless in prayers.

"It's no use!" Jess got up cranky and tired. "Who can sleep during all this?"

An evil little voice mimicked Jess's words. Then suddenly the voice became louder, stronger and much more horrifying in cruelty and wickedness.

"Mom!" Jess cried out.

"It's all right, Jess. Come have something to eat. We have to keep our strength up. Let us give great thanks to God for all He has given to us and for being so watchful of us, protecting us these past couple of days."

"Your days are about to come to a swift end!" a raving evil spirit spurted out.

John came close to his little family hugging them, trying to comfort them and keep warm, for it was so very cold.

"Why don't I read, while you both eat," John suggested seeing the both of them so weak and drained.

Joanne smiled at him, encouraging him too.

"I'll begin with St. Peter's . . ." John tried to begin but a loud crash startled them and John nearly dropped the book. He cleared his throat as if it was commonplace to hear loud crashes and continued anyway.

"Beloved: Be all like-minded in prayer, compassionate, lovers of the brethren, merciful, reserved, humble; not rendering evil for evil, or abuse for abuse, but contrariwise, blessing; for unto this were you called that you might inherit a blessing. For, 'He who would love life, and see good days, let him refrain his tongue from evil, and his lips that they speak no deceit. Let him turn away from evil and do good, let him seek after peace and pursue it. For the eyes of the Lord are upon the just, and . . .'"

Great crashes of thunder could be heard crashing everywhere! Joanne and Jess both jumped up with fright and screamed hearing those loud claps!

"What is happening now?" Jess asked her mother.

Joanne was shaking with fear, "I'm not sure, baby. It sounds as though the chastisement is becoming quite fierce out there."

John looked up too, "Maybe because we're coming to an end of all this soon. Hell doesn't have that much more time to . . ."

All at once more terrifying crashes and claps of thunder could be heard amongst whirlwinds of colossal proportions right outside their door.

"It sounds as though there are cyclones of fire burning and destroying everything we have ever . . ."

There came fierce poundings at their door.

John continued his reading, ". . . and His ears unto their prayers; but the face of the Lord is against those who do evil.' And who is there to harm you, if you are zealous for what is good? But even if you suffer anything for justice' sake, blessed are you. So have no fear of their fear and do not be troubled. But hallow the Lord Christ in your hearts."

"When will this be over? When will we be able to have silence again?" Joanne cried out.

There came no relief. The torture of so much violence raging constantly for days had surely taken its toll on many. People all over the world were worried, filled with anxiety, and trembling with fears as they tried to survive the wrath of God!

"Who is like unto God?" John blurted out hearing the wails of thousands outside their door.

"Poor Jill. How are they coping with a baby and so many kids? Think how hard it must be for them, for all our friends and neighbors. Think how lucky we are to have each other to comfort and encourage. What about those who are alone through all this? Poor wretched souls who are suffering this alone!" Joanne bowed her head.

"If I were alone I'd never make it through," Jess held tight to her mother.

"I'm grateful I had the sense to recognize what was happening and get home in time, before the commencement of all this. What if you never opened the door for me?" John shuttered to think.

"Come nearer to us, honey," Joanne held her hand out to her husband.

As John approached to where Joanne and Jess were seated his eyes widened in terror and disbelief! There before him were two of the most hideous creatures he had ever seen in his life! His heart began to speed up and he could almost hear himself sweat. Those eyes that stared back at him made him freeze in his tracks. Where were his wife and daughter? How had these foes gotten inside? Were his eyes playing tricks on him?

Chapter 12

The stench, the noise, the unrest, our hunger and the quest to pursue that which was righteous and avoid that which was evil was taking a great toll on all of us. We were failing in our endeavors trying to keep up with prayers, for we had never prayed so long or as earnestly as we had done the past couple of days.

The blending of the spiritual world into our world, the unknown seething into our physical world, was mind boggling. Angels of light were patrolling our streets while legions of demons scattered in every direction bent on destroying everything in their paths. God's wrath is terrible! Who is like unto God? Who would dare to look upon it? No one was prepared for these days even at the direction of Father's sermons. Though we had all made the little revisions we were told to prepare for, putting canned foods and blankets in a room with no windows, it was hardly preparation for what we had come face to face with.

Where was our leader? Where was Father McGrath? What was happening to him? And then getting a sudden chill, I began to think he must be going through an even greater torture, being a religious. How fiercely the devils must hate those servants of the Lord. I shuttered to think how enraged those wicked foes must have been in their efforts to make him falter, purposefully seeking first and foremost his ruination.

It was a lonely sight, an abandoned rectory in the middle of town. Father was one of those poor souls left alone to combat the demons. But besides his fears of them, he was fearful for his whole congregation, wondering how people were faring and if many had perished in their disbeliefs.

Prayers were commonplace for Father McGrath. He had always recited his Office prayers daily and said Mass each and every day. Rosaries were old hat. And ejaculations to his guardian angel and the great Mother of God came naturally for him. It took no effort to continue these routines, but it was growing hard to concentrate for days. In the wicked days we were going through, prayers needed to be said from the heart and with great devotion. Father, in the past, had sometimes become easily distracted during long vigils such as these.

Nonetheless, he bucked up and prayed sincerely and contritely, forcing the devils to scatter on many occasions, until the next attack was launched to try and upset his well regulated temperance. He glanced over at the blessed candle still burning brightly but nearly two thirds burned down. This was the only measure of time, which was slowly running out for all of hell, poor men, and what was left of our world.

Having finished his Office prayers and a fifteen decade rosary, Father turned his sights towards meditation. Wondering what had happened to his church, to his people and to the building itself, he began to weep, for he was such a loving person. And in that time of weeping the enemy regrouped and launched yet another attack.

But Father's heart was so magnanimous the clamors at the doorway and roof hardly phased him any longer. His fears were beginning to fade. And his love was overpowering. He began to pray for those who would not, for those too frightened to pray, for those who were too weary and tired, also for those most in need. He began to realize the last stages of the prophecy, that people would amend their ways and turn back to worship and adore God as it should be. He realized that the earth needed to be purified and made like new, that men had sinned far too much and for far too long. This chastisement had to come. There was no other way to make men amend their lives.

He began to recall the Fatima messages, relating to wars and other chastisements, realizing men were in need of warnings, but that even in hearing this news some did not heed it. He thought of people in his congregation one by one saying special prayers for them and prostrating to the ground in humbleness. Yes, this was the way of a servant of the Lord, to humble oneself and have a heart full of charity. But not only did the priests need to humble themselves, so likewise did all of mankind, with hearts full of charity for one another as well.

He recalled the rush of trips to so many people's homes to deliver holy water and blessed candles. He even blessed everything in the church bookstore, since people had bought up statues and such for added devotion and protection during these dreadful days. He loved the work he did realizing it was most pleasing to our Lord.

He thought of our weary family adding a few extra prayers especially for our little ones, knowing they would be terrified as we all were. He couldn't imagine the fears in those innocent little eyes. How would people see their children through it all? Or had many children perished, to spare them from the unbearable anguish that had engulfed the world? He wondered who was left in the world. When all of this was over, would he be alone and without anyone near him for miles and miles?

His thoughts turned to the Sullivan family too. There were so many children in their household. Did Mrs. Sullivan make enough revisions for their sustenance? How was Mr. Sullivan coping? Was there still law and order in their house? What about their James, the mischievous little rascal that was always fidgeting in church, how was he doing?

Next he reflected on the Nelson's. He had gotten word about Don breaking his leg. Perhaps it wasn't too bad for him. All he needed to do was lay prostrate on the floor or sit in a chair. He knew Margaret would be taking special care of him.

He thought about the Nelson's neighbors. What were their names? Who were they? Oh yes, the King family. What had become of the Kings who wouldn't heed their advice to keep blessed candles in their home and get ready for a most grueling event? He shuttered just to think of their demise.

After praying for each and every family in his care, Father turned his thoughts to Heaven and began to meditate on the works of our Lady and our Lord. How often They had sent messages to mankind through apparitions to the saints, in the changes of nature and in so many other ways. He thought about how full the gospels are in lessons and wisdom. If man had only taken heed. Just to read the Bible a little every day, one would learn it contained great blessings and indulgences. Why did it need to take such a catastrophe for men to open this book?

Suddenly his thoughts were elevated, and he turned to the metaphysical, overloaded with questions as to why all these things were taking place. But those deeper questions, needing such profound answers, would be answered at a later date.

What was the purpose of man? What path was he supposed to tread on? Why had he swayed from righteousness? Would these three dark days be enough to steer him back? Would men really amend their ways? And if so, for how long?

How long after this chastisement would men forget about it and start back to the path of destruction? Two, three, four generations from now, would the world still be rid of its vulgarities?

The blessed candle was the beacon of light in his little cell. The room burned brightly under its white haze. Father grabbed for an extra blanket. It was still so terribly cold and seeming to grow even colder as there was no sunlight to heat the world now for days. He continued his pious thoughts until exhaustion over took him and he soon fell off to sleep.

The chaos outside in the darkness roared to new heights. Time was running out for hell and the destruction of mankind and destroying the world was the only agenda the demons sought to undertake with all their might.

But a new battle was brewing, that which involved Almighty God and the angels of light. Slowly, with great precision and strength these heavenly armies moved forward forcing the demons to take flight and abandon their wicked tasks. Loud wails and terrible lamentation could be heard for miles as the devils were forced to surrender under the powerful hand of God! Even the valleys shook with fear!

Father McGrath was exhausted. The demons had been unmerciful to him. But his love and wisdom, his knowledge of the faith, saw him through it all. At long last it was ending. As he sank in slumber, he began to dream of what the new world would be like, wondering if there would be any semblance to the old world that had just been purged.

His thoughts went back in time to the creation of the world and he saw the great plans God had taken to create a world for mankind in the corner of the universe. From the darkness came the light. From nothingness came the planets and stars. Amidst the whirlwinds of the Mighty Hands of God came forth life of so many kinds. Water was separated from the lands. Creatures of every shape and size came forth. Plants and vegetation grew for medicinal purposes, to eat, and to give back to the land. There was order in this great process. Each creature having a purpose, each form of life played off of the next, each creation fitted into a perfect balance. And when all had been accomplished God created man and woman.

And it was given to man that he should have dominion over the land. The world was his to live peacefully in and to prosper. There was only one warning given, a warning to obey. But soon enough, this was ignored and man fell into sin and hardships. And from that first fall came many other falls. It became the nature of man to sin even until the present day.

So many sins, so many falls, so many offenses to God brought about the *Three Days of Darkness*. We were deserving of this punishment. We had been warned so many times by the prophets of a great chastisement to come. Now it was here, purging the world of its sins.

But the end results, after the punishment was over, promised to be different. It was going to be just like paradise, as if we were starting all over again. The world would be rid of all its corruption. Cyclones of fire were sent to destroy the arrogance of men. Demons were being allowed to swallow up men who had scoffed at God's warnings, men who thought they were above the events that came to be, men who had sinned and had not repented.

Oceans were boiling up spitting out the sunken ships and carcasses of wayward men once lost at sea. The universe was being shaken and the patterns of stars and planets were being rearranged. The new formation of the world was almost completed. When all of that was in order mankind, what was left of him, would come out into a new world order.

Father trembled in his sleep. Loud poundings persisted at his door. The blessed candle was slowly burning down.

"Who is like unto God?" he shouted out from his slumbers, observing all these transformations.

And then Father looked into the spiritual realm. He saw Heaven and the creation of the angels. He saw Lucifer, a radiant beautiful angel of light! But then Lucifer, loving his own beauty more than serving God, fell from grace. And in falling became more ugly and more horrid than any creature ever created. As the wicked serpent fell he dragged with him legions of other angels who also had become corrupt and into the fiery abyss and the caverns of hell they all fell.

The ruination of Lucifer and those other fallen angels wasn't enough. Once man was created in the image and likeness of God, Lucifer became obsessed with destroying men who merely looked like God, though he could never destroy God Himself. His course of action to get even with God preoccupied his imagination relentlessly. And ignorant men, so fragile in their surroundings, so inferior to angels and their high intelligence, were fair game. And so at the first opportunity a serpent was sent to seduce the weaker of mankind, namely the first woman.

Father began to wail, "No, don't talk to him! Don't listen!"

But it was already too late. With the fall of Eve came the closing to the gates of Heaven. Perhaps that was why it was also forewarned not to talk or pay heed to anyone outside the doors and windows during the *Three Days of Darkness*! Just to communicate with those evil forces was the beginning of being caught off guard and soon falling into the careful traps they always have planned. The focus should always be to God! God is the Rescuer! He is the Source from which men gain strength and the Only Means by which men can be saved!

Father awoke with a start hearing someone at the door! He reached for his trusty bottle of holy water and not even giving it another thought splashed an ample amount all over the windows and door. A vapor rose about the dwelling place and a fowl stench nearly made him gag. He had scattered rose petals at the base of a statue of the Blessed Virgin in his room. As he made his way over to her, he picked up a few of the lovely petals in his hand, and placing them under his nostrils breathed in the goodness of their smell. He got back down on the floor, prostrating before the image, and began the Litany prayers to the Blessed Virgin Mary.

Poor Father, so terribly exhausted, soon drifted back off to sleep. His dreaming resumed as he began to see the history of mankind looming before him. What would become of the history we had known? Would everything be erased so that we could begin anew? Or perhaps history would need to be rewritten, when all was said and done.

He saw the building of the great pyramids in Egypt! He watched the architects and surveyors at work. He could see noble men, riding their fine chariots, coming to see their progress. He watched the artisans craft their sculptures of gold and turquoise for elaborate burial masks for the pharaohs who would one day be covered by them. He knew of their plans to mummify these noble men and lower them into heavy sarcophaguses, placing them inside these magnificent architectural dwellings. He watched men chisel and build the magnificent statues in the Valley of the Kings and at the Sphinx. For centuries these great works had stood as a reminder of a past race.

Then Father trembled, thinking perhaps during these difficult times, those great monuments were falling to ruins. Nonetheless, they were being shown to him just as they had occurred in time.

He was transported to ancient Greece where he watched the great buildings being erected on top of the Acropolis. One after the other the Parthenon, the Erechtheion and the Caryatids were built. He saw the beginnings of paganism and the temples built to worship their false gods, such as the Temple of the Olympian Zeus and the Hephaistos Temple.

He saw the great Agamemnon tomb, in Peloponnesus, the Lion Gate and the Theater in Epidaurus being built. He witnessed the erection of the Apollo Temple in Delphi taking form and the treasure-house of the Athenians.

Transported to all the corners of the world he saw the building of Stonehenge and the great mathematical mysteries attached to this fortress revealed in its own time. He saw the pyramids in the jungles of Mexico, Chichen Itza and Tulum, marveling at the skills and precisions of our ancient ancestors. Would all of these marvels still be standing when the sun was allowed to shine again after the *Three Days of Darkness*?

He saw the reigns, the rise and fall, of many pharaohs, kings and noblemen. He saw the triumphs and defeats of great empires, one after the other. He witnessed the births and the deaths of Moses, Ramses II, Nefertari, Cleopatra, Caesar and more. Time and events were being played back to Father over in his mind as if it were some sort of picture show. He could fathom the minds of these men and saw how reckless some of them had become, drunk with power and greed.

Rome in particular became one of the most powerful civilizations, and he could see the rise and fall of this empire, even witnessing the tragedy at Pompeii. He witnessed all these things and saw the restlessness of men and the many sins each had committed, until a very quiet night befell the earth, and a star or a comet appeared over a cave in Bethlehem.

A Saviour had been born! And in that same district there was a great peace. But peace was not to prevail for long. Even in the stillness of that holy night, great wicked plans were being devised to execute the lives of the first born all over this region. The sorcerers had forewarned that there would be One born among them Who would rise to a very high standing position. These paranoid and vulgar rulers, frightened that their wicked days were numbered, sent forth a decree to kill the first born in each family. Perhaps by eliminating this threat of some great new leader this would ensure their thrones to be filled only by unruly men such as themselves. St. Joseph took his holy family and fled to Egypt.

Countless miracles and prophecies later, Father stood watching at the foot of a Cross the tragic yet triumphant crucifixion of our Lord Jesus Christ. Sins had finally been forgiven with the death of our Lord and Heaven's gates were once again opened to mankind.

But would man be grateful? How long would it take to wean off this sweetest of miracles or rather return to a life of more power and greed, of lust and adultery, of avarice and paganism? Not very long at all.

Many centuries passed, they came and went. Constantine, St. Augustine of Hippo, and Charlemagne, all rose to power and then expired in the blink of an eye, no more than whispers in the wind. The ancient church struggled for acknowledgement under constant attacks. Heresies loomed up against her. Saints and prophets were sent to defend the early church, some even died for her. But Lucifer never tired in his relentless quest to destroy this divine institution.

The years of barbarianism and the early days of Christianity had their own problems and punishments. Medieval times, the middle ages, and the Renaissance all contributed to the way of man's thinking bringing him further away from God as he sought his own perception of the truth.

Man's world suddenly turned against him, bringing with it misery and death, with the Black Plague. But a worst predicament befell mankind when the church began splitting down the middle and dividing each member one against the other. How could this reformation have come to be?

Great Popes intervened drawing up important papers and decrees, hoping to put an end to the rampant destruction of what was holy and worth retaining for the generations who would follow. But these preparations would prove useless to a destructive mankind who worked diligently to destroy what the forefathers had left them!

With the discovery of the telescope, exploration, and the excursions to a new land came the quests for freedom and to live a life free to worship as men chose. Napoleon came and went. George Washington, Lincoln, Roosevelt, Churchill, Hitler and Reagan had their moments. But it was like that of a passing breeze, each man had no more than a little place in the realm of things.

Had mankind learned any significant lessons? Were we drawing from the example of our Saviour or were we running off wildly to pursue life in a manner less structured from Christ's teachings? No one seemed to sit down and think about it much.

And then suddenly during the 1800's they began. People from all over Europe, from Spain, from Belgium, Italy and France began circulating a warning of a great chastisement that was about to befall all the earth. Seers, saints and blesseds one by one described the chastisement that was at hand. Similarities began to arise. And soon they were all categorized into one great prophecy that became better known as the *Three Days of Darkness*!

Towards the later part of the 1800's apparitions of the Blessed Mother commenced first at LaSalette, France in 1846, then at Lourdes, France in 1858 and then later again at Fatima, Portugal in 1917. Another apparition was reported in Akita, Japan in October 1973. Messages of doom came with these apparitions and warnings. A great chastisement was about to befall mankind.

"What were those messages? Why weren't they completely revealed to mankind as was asked by the most Blessed Virgin Mary? What boldness of men to ignore the Mother of God!

"Who defies the great Mother of God?" Father called out in his sleep.

Quietly and purposefully the messages were suppressed and forgotten, for what purpose we do not know. Then many other countries began to point to spots where seers had seen visions of the Blessed Mother.

"Look she's in Spain on this mountain!"

"Now she's in New York, USA at the old World's Fair!"

"She's here!"

"She's there!"

"Where do we turn?"

It was made clear to Father that if anyone was looking for the truth there was one source to find it. Through the history of mankind there was only one book that told a story of the truth, that book being the Bible. But this good book had also become an instrument for controversy at the split during the Reformation and again at another split during the 1960's. Chapters were deleted, names were changed, verses were lost in translations, things were added and much was taken away.

Father tossed and turned having before his eyes the remains of the Catholic Church.

Vatican II had virtually destroyed the solemnness of the Mass by rewriting all its prayers. This council opened the door for countless other changes. Having the door open to changes, another Pope decided to make additions to the rosary as if the Blessed Mother had made some mistake in manufacturing it for St. Dominic centuries ago.

Once the faith was weakened, men who are naturally weak would fall. Men needed guidance and the church of the forefather's had always offered them that. But holy church was too mixed up to lead them now.

Priests were struggling, some persevering and trying to preserve the faith, while others pursued more worldly pleasures and conquests of power. The church had been reduced to a remnant, which is why the chastisement was long overdue in setting things straight.

Father began to weep, then he lamented. Many had been caught off guard, not expecting such a catastrophe to occur in their lifetime. Nor did they ever dream their gods would do them any harm. Still, most of the world didn't know what hit them! So many had already been lost in a world of lies and deceits. They weren't prepared for the destruction foretold. So few had heard anything about it.

Who had time to study their faith? It was such a bother to go to church or to worship. Sundays were fun days to go shopping at the mall or meet the girls for brunch or go fishing for that perfect bluefish! Maybe every once in a while some people would make it to church, just to meet up with friends, so that they could plan something afterwards. No one took their religion seriously anymore. There were far too many other things going on that were more important anyway.

The gates of hell were opening every day wider and wider getting ready for its due of poor souls!

"They didn't know," Father wept, "They didn't know . . ."

Besides his struggle to understand why so many had perished, he began to rethink what fate awaited those who had made it through the ordeal.

"How will we be able to clean up all the remains? What stench will there be with so many corpses? Or will the ocean engulf them, washing the lands clean of all their putrid bodies? How will we eat? What foods will be left unscathed? Will the pestilence and poisonous fumes released into the air from the bowels of hell pollute our world even after the wake of a new day? Or will the remains of all that has occurred be forced back to its proper place in hell?"

Many, many questions came to mind in Father's head. He prostrated in deep thankfulness, for being one of the priests who had been spared, in a world that had been so full of wicked men. And he humbled himself not believing he had ever been worthy enough to be one of those who would be saved.

"Where will we begin? How will we begin again?" he cried out.

The next thing Father knew he had awakened to a most horrifying howl right outside his door! He had been enlightened by his dreaming and as he reached for his jug of holy water, to refresh his door and cleanse it, he began to rethink all the history of mankind over again in his mind.

"Yes, the new world will need a new way of life! They will need to turn back to God! They will need guidance and the truth. How will they know which way to follow unless it is written down for them? They will need the whole Bible, with correct names and places in it, without deletions of any kind! They will need to know the history of mankind, so that hopefully they can proceed to live life not having to repeat its mistakes." Father arose looking for some paper and a pen so that he could write this all down.

Furious roars and great claps of thunder echoed throughout the rectory as it shook to its very foundations!

"There will be no more big businesses, which means there won't be anymore supermarkets. There won't be gas stations or mass transportation. No big companies will run the power plants. What will become of electricity and running water? How will those that are left learn about all these things? What if no libraries are left after these *Three Days of Darkness* are over?"

Father splashed his door with holy water, echoing just as loud as the evil beings outside there in the darkness, "Let God arise, and let His enemies be scattered, and let them that hate Him flee from before His face!"

Not only was the world being chastised and purged, but also the religious were undergoing a terrific elimination of false priests, false leaders and false prophets! The Lord was cleansing His church as well! There would be no evil left in a purified world!

Chapter 13

"Why are you anxious? Consider how the lilies of the field grow; they neither toil nor spin, yet I say to you that not even Solomon in all his glory was arrayed like one of these. But if God so clothes the grass of the field, which flourishes today but tomorrow is thrown into the oven, how much more you, O you of little faith! Therefore do not be anxious, saying, *'What shall we eat?'* or, *'What shall we drink?'* or, *'What are we to put on?'* (for after all these things the Gentiles seek); for your Father knows that you need all these things. But seek first the kingdom of God and His justice, and all these things shall be given you besides," Rick looked up from his reading, and over to me, then to Kate who was beginning to have a crying fit.

Baby Kate was thirsty for more juice. I quickly filled another bottle for her from a juice box and lovingly fed it to her. She had come so far, having gone through so much. And still she seemed a happy and healthy baby. God had mercifully spared her, and the rest of us too!

"Let us give thanks to God for leading us onward and protecting us during these most trying times!" I smiled warmly on my family.

It was also said loud enough for the demons to become enraged! And the reason for this horrific uproar was because Lucifer's legions were agitated that their time to devour mankind and destroy the world was slowly running out. With little time to go, each demon's crash and bang at the door, and on the ceiling, and from all around us, became louder and done more angrily.

But for us, we had become more confident in our prayers and had become strengthened with fortitude with every attack launched at us. Our angels, the Blessed Mother of God, and God Himself had seen us through our trials and protected each of us through these most horrific three days.

I looked over to my husband, then to my children, all tired and drained. But this was not the time to rest, not just yet. The demon's, knowing we were all worn out, were anxious for a slip-up and eagerly awaited whatever opportunity that might come their way. The final day was the most grueling of all the days for all mankind, because we had been tested to our limits thus far.

"How much longer mommy, will the devils keep making those noises?" little Ricky asked me shivering from the cold.

"Not much longer now, not much more time left at all," I brought him near to me and huddled with him beneath an over-sized blanket.

"Lay prostrate, each of you," I instructed my children. "If it's possible, try to get a little sleep."

Then Rick smiled at me, "Let's pray the rosary. In the name of the Father, and of the Son, and of the Holy Ghost . . ."

Mary Alice Sullivan was wrapping her brothers in extra blankets, "This has to be the coldest day of all!"

Everyone was shivering and trying to be brave.

Mr. Sullivan put his arms around his wife and told the rest of the children to huddle closer together also, "Our body heat will help us to stay warm."

"Keep praying," Mrs. Sullivan echoed.

Just then, Patrick and Edward began a scuffle tugging and pulling the blankets.

Chris continued with his reading aloud, "Bear one another's burdens, and so you will fulfill the law of Christ. For if anyone thinks himself to be something, whereas he is nothing, he deceives himself. But let everyone test his own work, and so he will have glory in himself only, and not in comparison with another. For each one will bear his own burden. And let him who is instructed in the word share all good things with his teacher. Be not deceived, God is not mocked . . ."

"Patrick, please!" Mrs. Sullivan was near tears. "We must pull together in all this! Share with your brother! Let this be a lesson to come closer to each other, not drive you apart!"

Mr. Sullivan chimed in as well, "Have we not learned anything these past two days? When will the lesson be learned?"

A great roar of laughter issued forth from every corner of the house. Then in a mocking sort of fashion the evil spirits took turns repeating, "Have we not learned anything these past two days? Have we not learned anything?" Each demon took his turn to provoke the little family all the more, knowing their anxieties and their shortcomings.

Mr. Sullivan looked over to Chris who was shivering and tired, huddled in the corner. He got up and went over to him, took the book from his hands, and patted his head. He nodded to his son to go over with the rest of the family and cuddle together to get warm. Then Mr. Sullivan resumed the reading himself opening the book to the page Chris had just left off from.

"For what a man sows, that he will also reap. For he who sows in the flesh, from the flesh also will reap corruption. But he who sows in the spirit, from the spirit will reap life everlasting. And in doing good let us not grow tired; for in due time we shall reap if we do not relax. Therefore, while we have time, let us do good to all men, but especially to those who are of the household of faith."

A great crackling and loud crashing came from outside! Loud moans and deep pitiful wails came forth from the top of the evil one's lungs! Hell was being driven back. They were loosing the battle. They were being cast down into the abyss. This was the most horrific battle of all!

☙❧

Jess huddled close to her mother and father, "I'm so cold! Will it ever be warm again?"

John took them both in his arms, "Not too much longer now. Soon this will all be over. It's going to be a better world. We're going to see a new promised land. We're so close now. Just imagine it . . ."

Joanne was crying.

"It's all right, mommy. I'm not cold anymore. I can see it, dad. I can imagine the world all sparkling and shiny new!"

"You'll *never* see another good thing you miserable creature! I'll make certain of that myself!" a deep gruffy voice breathed into the woodwork.

Joanne grabbed hold of them tighter. She was so drained, so very tired. "Were going to make it with the help of our angels. Let's pray to them. Oh angels of God, our Guardians dear. To whom God's love, commits us here. Ever this day, be at our sides. To light and guide, to rule and guide, Amen."

"And let us continue praying, never leaving off," John interjected. He knew the value of sincere prayers. "And who

is there to harm you, if you are zealous for what is good? But
even if you suffer anything for justice' sake, blessed are you. So
have no fear of their fear and do not be troubled. But hallow
the Lord Christ in your hearts."

Baby Kate had fallen back to sleep. Who would have thought
that little one could sleep through all the noise? Perhaps
running the vacuum cleaner with the television on, and the
phone ringing, and the kids running around the house all those
days before these dreadful days, was good experience for her.
Rachel too had drifted off in slumber on my lap. Daniel and
Ricky huddled close to their father. And Rick and I looked at
one another lip sinking the rosary one Ave after another.

We both were worried. Neither of us knew what lay ahead
of us. Would there really be a Garden of Eden, a paradise,
awaiting us with the cleansing completed? How would we
provide for our children? Would there be the heat of the sun?
Would there be wood for fire? Would we find water? Would
the land be suitable for planting? Where would we find seeds?
Would we find our neighbors alive? Would there be any other
survivors? Hundreds of questions raced through our minds
and I felt a sense of hopelessness. I was ready to give up the
fight.

"We're going to make it," Rick smiled across the little
laundry room to me.

I burst into tears.

"We've come this far, we're not about to give up now!
We have fought the good fight. We have been earnest in our
prayers. We have believed in the power of God and of all things
good. We have had the assistance of the Blessed Mother, our
angels, and the saints. And in our hardest times they never
abandoned us."

The devils roared in anger at his words, "You'll never see
the light of day again!" And each one climbed over the next

demon clawing and scratching at the worn out little door, still very eager to destroy all of us who were huddled safe inside our little room.

The children also began to cry. Rick was showing he was worn out too but shouldered his weakness by softly singing out, "When you walk through the storm, hold your head up high and don't be afraid of the storm . . ."

He continued to sing as the devils seemed to scatter running and banging on the walls outside. I looked up with a start wondering what was taking place. Were those demons really retreating or were they contriving a new plan of attack eager to come back to destroy us with? Rick continued to sing, louder and louder, until there was no more commotion outside the door.

"They're regrouping!" I whispered. "Everyone get ready!"

We weren't sure what new tactic the demons would use, but Rick and I knew this would be the greatest attack, since it was perhaps their last chance to harm us. We braced ourselves as we huddled close to one another ready for anything.

And then it happened. Slowly a sound I shall never forget began to pierce the frightful stillness. It was that of a rushing sound like a fierce wind or the sound of water rushing. It was ubiquitous. The children quickly covered their ears and huddled all the more closely together. Rick's face filled with alarm, and as the sound grew louder and louder rushing at us, I too covered my ears.

"This is it!" Rick shouted. "Stay together! I love you all!"

It was as if we were all on the fiercest of all roller coasters at this point. The room seemed to lift us and twirl us in the most horrid of fashions. We were slammed and thrown bumping and sprawled about as if we were dolls tossed in playing. The children cried out in horror! I tried with all my might to grasp out and hold onto them. But I could not hold onto anything except my rosary.

"Grasp and hold tight to your rosaries!" I shouted.

And then came the most frightening sounds of all, demons in distress! The wails and anguish of all of hell being pushed back into their abyss, in great defeat, was horrific!

"Cover your ears!" Rick screamed at us.

The sounds made all of us cry of great fear! The children appeared to be lifeless. They had fainted. And Rick and I cried as if we too would faint or not make it through this suffering. I looked over to my husband as if this was the last time I would ever see him again. This was it. It was all over now. I could bear no more horror and no more punishment. I was about to close my eyes and part the world. My eyelids burdened with tears and heaviness began to close. I resigned myself to my angel and sank back against the wall.

Rick could see me fading and cried out, "No!"

But it didn't seem to matter at that point. I had never been so frightened at anything before in all my life. I had had enough. And Rick, thinking I was dying, swooned himself. We had all been tested to our limits.

As his eyes began to shut as well the last thing that he saw through half closed lids was the blessed candle. It had burned for three days and was ready to extinguish itself. And then the candle went out!

Rick at this point had given up, but then something strange began to take place. There was a dreadful stillness, almost as frightening as it had been when the demons departed to regroup for another attack. Yet this stillness was different. We had not heard this type of stillness since our ordeal had begun.

Rick cried out to me, "Jill . . . Jill hang on." He struggled to lift himself and open his eyes. He strained to focus on the room we were in and on the children and me. He could see us, in the darkness, without the candle! That meant there would have to be light! Turning to look at the little wooden door he saw a faint light coming from beneath it!

It was the same with the Sullivan family. They too had been jolted and thrown about their room. They too had heard that most dreadful of all cries from hell. They too had screamed out in disbelief and anguish. Some of them had fainted for fear!

Chris was the first to notice the blessed candle that he never took his eyes off of. He struggled to get closer to it and have a better look. It had burned down in the glass container to its bottom. There were only a few little drops of wax left in it. It was flickering, ready to go out. And then it did!

Chris rushed at it in terror and disbelief! "We've been faithful! We've prayed so hard! We can not be forsaken!" He picked up the glass jar and shook it as if it needed batteries and hoped with all hopes that it would turn back on again. But it did not.

"God save us!" he threw the empty jar against the wall.

Mr. Sullivan hearing the crashing of glass raised his lowered heavy head. He too was ready to give up the fight. His children huddled together in groups about the room. His wife had either died or had passed out from fear. He surely felt that all was now lost. Then, very subtly, a small ray of light began to filter in from beneath their doorway. Colleen noticed it first and then Mary Alice.

"Look!" Colleen gasped and pointed.

"Great Mother of God!" Mr. Sullivan looked keenly in the direction of the light. "Maureen, wake up! Please, please Maureen, you have to see this!" Mr. Sullivan tried with all his might to reach for his wife who had been thrown nearly half way across the room.

The children huddled together, "Perhaps this is a trick!"

"Maybe the devils have planned this so that we'll go outside!"

"They're trying to trick us again, I say!"

"Don't go near the door. It's part of another wicked plan!"

Mr. Sullivan composed himself becoming tearful with great hope and a renewed joy, "No, this is not a trick. The blessed candle has burned out after three days! The wax was the measure and now it is gone! The chastisement is over! At long last, it is over! What fate awaits us now?" He reached for his wife and took her in his arms weeping for relief and great joy.

There was a great silence that filled the room where they were gathered. Mrs. Sullivan slowly opened her eyes and gazed lovingly at her husband.

Joanne was the first to crawl up from the floor where a chair had pinned her against the side wall. She was worried about Jess and John. They were crouched near the corner, on the far opposite end of the room, still shaking with fear. Neither of them moved. They were focused on their blessed candle. Joanne reached to preserve it, seeing it flicker, but to no avail. The flame went out!

Her hand fell swiftly to the floor. She was exhausted from the ordeal and had no more strength left to even move any further. John was so shaken he stayed put where he was still holding Jess who had her face buried in his chest. His eyes were popping out of his skull as he looked on in terror that their blessed candle had been extinguished!

They were so afraid they did not notice the rays of light beginning to stream in from beneath their doorway.

Father McGrath had nearly given up all hope also, when suddenly he noticed his candle flame go out and a deafening silence fill the rectory. The candle had been his focus the entire three days knowing it was like a clock to measure how long the chastisement would last. He knew at once that the ordeal was over. The wax was gone. The three days had been fulfilled.

He was anxious to open the door to his room. The door had protected him for three days against the wickedness and snares of the devil. Now upon opening it, the door would lead him into a new world, one of peace and great love. This was the promise and the ending to the prophecy. He rose up from his chair shaking and wobbly. Fixing his hair and picking up the Good Book he walked across the room and put this hand to the doorknob. Slowly carefully he opened it.

The children awoke one right after the other. First baby Kate who was the most resilient, then Rachel, then Daniel and Ricky. Each of them opened and rubbed their eyes. My arm was aching having been thrown against a wall and landing on it. I tried to flex it and immediately reached for my children to hug and reassure them.

"It's over!" Rick sighed in great relief. He launched across the room to us and we all held and hugged one another with the greatest of compassion. We all started to cry.

"There is light outside," Rick reiterated. "We have to go out there and see what kind of world we now live in."

I grabbed even more tightly to my children, "What if it's a trick? How will we know it is safe?"

"I'll go first," Rick assured us.

"No, daddy! Don't go out there!" Ricky screamed. Then everyone began to cry again.

"It's all right. There, there. The blessed candle is used up. It was foretold to us that it would not go out in the houses of the faithful. It burned all its wax for us. Now that it has gone out, we know it is over. We will need food and have to begin all over again with whatever lies in store for us out there. I will go first and make sure everything is all right. I will come back for you if this is the case. Wait here and keep praying. Don't come out until I return," Rick kissed each of the children on their foreheads. Then he turned to me and with tears in his eyes he whispered, "I love you."

We embraced as if for the last time weeping but happy things had become normal again.

"Cover your eyes. Don't look out this door until I tell you to do so," Rick commanded us.

We each did as we were told.

"This is it! God be with me!" and with his hand on the doorknob Rick slowly and purposely opened the door to our little room. He stepped outside. We kept in our places covering our eyes. The door closed peacefully behind him. There was no commotion heard.

"Daddy! Daddy!" the children cried out.

"It's all right. Shhh, be quiet. Let's listen," I tried to tell them.

We heard nothing. No commotion. No sounds of war. No disturbances of any kind. Just then the children jumped with joy. They heard the sounds of birds.

"Listen, mommy!" Rachel cried out. "Do you hear the birds singing?"

"Yes," I strained to hear. "Yes, I do."

But we waited, doing what we had been instructed to do. It seemed like an eternity later when Rick finally returned and opened the door coming back inside. I jumped up to embrace him crying and laughing into his shoulder.

The children ran to greet him as well.

"Look at daddy's face!" Daniel pointed out.

I slowly stepped back to have a look.

John embraced Jess and Joanne before he too made the decision to venture outside and assess the damages. "I'll be all right. Just stay here until I come back. Keep the windows and doors covered just in case. I'm not sure what I'll find out there."

"Take your rosaries with you," Joanne handed them to him and embraced him with Jess.

He slowly opened the door to their room and went outside closing it carefully behind him.

Joanne and Jess huddled together crying inside.

The Sullivans voted on who would be the one to explore outside. Mrs. Sullivan was still too weak from the ordeal so she was not considered for this exploration. It was decided that Chris would go. Mr. Sullivan embraced his son with tears in his eyes and patted his back as he watched him head for the door.

"I know you'll be back soon, son! Godspeed you!" Then Mr. Sullivan turned to the rest of his family and quickly told them to cover their eyes. The door to the little room was opened.

Father McGrath didn't know what he would find but had mustered up the fortitude to step outside. What he found was unbelievable. He stood there at the doorway of the rectory spellbound and in a state of shock. He didn't move from that place for quite sometime. He didn't speak except to whisper, "Praise God!"

I looked up at my husband's face. It was a face glowing in a strange light, one that I had never seen before. He looked as though he looked upon something extraordinary, something not of the world, something we all too would soon look upon.

"Rick!" I shook him, "What is it? What's out there?"

He stood staring into space for a few seconds then he looked at all of us and broke down crying, "It's over! It's really over! Come with me! Come outside!"

We all cried together and huddled together. Then I reached for baby Kate and taking her in my arms followed my husband with our children to the door.

"Before we go outside we must thank God for seeing us through this horrific chastisement," Rick said.

All of us immediately got down on our knees and thanked God, the Blessed Mother Mary and all the angels and saints for their intercession and protection during those three most horrific days. We were all filled with a great sense of duty and piety, especially Rick, who had already been outside.

"All rise," Rick instructed us.

We all got up as we were told to do. I held tightly to baby Kate. The other children lined up at the door. Rick turned the knob and slowly opened the door to our hiding place. The door opened. Each of us one at a time stepped outside. As we all took our turns going outside, something we had not been able to do for three days, we all gasped at what we saw. There were no words to describe it. What we all saw with our own eyes was . . .

Made in United States
North Haven, CT
31 March 2022

17746821R00104